GRAVE DEEDS

Books by Betsy Struthers

Fiction:

Found: A Body. Toronto: Simon & Pierre, 1992

Poetry:

Running Out Of Time. Toronto: Wolsak & Wynn, 1993
Saying So Out Loud. Oakville: Mosaic, 1988
Censored Letters. Oakville: Mosaic, 1984

GRAVE DEEDS

BETSY STRUTHERS

Simon & Pierre
Toronto, Canada

Editor: Marian M. Wilson
Cover Illustration: Steve Raetsen
Printed and bound in Canada by Metrolitho Inc., Quebec

The writing of this manuscript and the publication of this book were made possible by support from several sources. We would like to acknowledge the generous assistance and ongoing support of **The Canada Council, The Book Publishing Industry Development Program** of the **Department of Canadian Heritage, The Ontario Arts Council,** and **The Ontario Publishing Centre** of the **Ministry of Culture, Tourism and Recreation.**

Kirk Howard, President; Marian M. Wilson, Publisher

Simon & Pierre Publishing Co. Ltd., a subsidiary of Dundurn Press

1 2 3 4 5 • 9 8 7 6 5

Canadian Cataloguing in Publication Data

Struthers, Betsy, 1951-
  Grave deeds

ISBN 0-88924-257-7

I. Title.

PS8587.T298G7 1993   C813'.54   C93-095037-2
PR9199.3.S77G7 1994

Order from Simon & Pierre Publishing Co. Ltd., care of

Dundurn Press Limited	**Dundurn Distribution**	**Dundurn Press Limited**
2181 Queen Street East	73 Lime Walk	1823 Maryland Avenue
Suite 301	Headington, Oxford	P.O. Box 1000
Toronto, Canada	England	Niagara Falls, N.Y.
M4L 1E5	0X3 7AD	U.S.A. 14302-1000

ACKNOWLEDGEMENTS

For their advice and assistance, I thank Constable Lynne Buehler, Peterborough Community Police Service; Kenneth Doherty, Manager, Peterborough Centennial Museum and Archives; and Dr. Susan Jamieson, Department of Anthropology, Trent University. Any errors are, of course, my own.

And as always, I thank Jim Struthers, my first best reader.

for my parents, L.H. Porter and Susanne E. Porter,
with love

ONE

The moment I turned the corner, I saw the crowd. About twenty people huddled together on the sidewalk halfway down the block, mostly women holding small children by the hand. In spite of the breeze blowing up from the lake, chilling the brightness of the spring sun, only a few wore jackets over casual sweatshirts and jeans. Their chatter competed with the squabble of starlings nesting among the new leaves of the maples that lined the street. A couple of elderly men stood in the centre of the road, one of them clutching the leash of a small fat terrier. Its high-pitched yaps were echoed by the excited barking of a Doberman whose head popped up periodically, as it threw itself against the tall wooden fence next door. Two boys on bicycles sped down the hill and screeched to a stop by the women. Voices rose and fingers pointed. A baby cried.

I stopped to consult the letterhead printed at the top of the thick creamy paper on which my aunt had sent me an invitation to visit. I hadn't known until she wrote that I had an aunt. My father left when I was still a baby; my mother died shortly after my marriage. I never met his relatives and hers were far away in England. As for my husband's family, well, you know how in-laws are. My lack of relations is only one of the things Will's mother holds against me. One of the smaller things at that.

The address matched the house; the letter didn't. Written in beautiful flowing script, the formal note of introduction and invitation induced those fantasies so familiar to my lonely child-hood: that I had been exchanged in the hospital at birth and that my real family were rich and loving and looking for me. Not that I didn't love my mother, but she worked long hours as a lawyer's secretary. I spent many dark winter afternoons sitting in the front windowseat of our apartment waiting for her to come home, and imagining a different life in a house full of siblings and grandparents.

This house was in a neighbourhood developed at the begin-ning of the century as a summer residence for the bourgeois of the city, those who wanted and could afford to escape the smell and congestion of downtown in exchange for the long white beaches at the end of a thirty-minute streetcar ride. It dated from that era: a frame cottage with gabled windows overlook-ing the roof of a verandah that wrapped around three of its sides. Once it had been painted white with dark green trim. What could be seen through the mass of ivy and overgrown bushes that pressed against the walls was gray weathered wood and boarded windows.

I joined the group of watchers, choosing to stand beside a woman my age who stood a little apart from the others, her feet still on the brick path that led to her own front door. She wore a faded pink track suit and new white running shoes; her graying hair was cut short. She didn't join in the excited specu-lation of her neighbours, but stared fiercely across at my aunt's house, her arms crossed tightly over her breasts, her eyes squinting against the sunlight or against tears — it was hard to tell which.

A hearse backed up the drive, crowding a police car onto a lawn of tall grass and dandelions. A white sedan was pulled up on the sidewalk. Red and white rooftop lights flickered in the brilliant spring sun. The crackle of radio static and the urgent repetition of a coded call echoed beneath the twittering of robins and the soothing coo of pigeons that strutted across the roof ridge between chimneys, craning their necks to see if any-one down below was about to throw them food. No one was.

A uniformed policeman stood on the verandah at the top of a flight of four steps. Two men in suits conferred on the threshold. They moved aside as the door swung open. For a moment, the attendant's back hid the gurney he was manoeuvring down the stairs.

A quiet groan rose when the body, wrapped in a blanket, came into view. The woman next to me sighed heavily and muttered half aloud, "So. That's that."

"Excuse me," I said. "What's happened here?"

My voice startled her. Her hands dropped to her sides, forming fists. She glared at me and, without answering, turned her back. I watched her stride into her house and winced at the crash of the slammed door.

A small gnarled and liver-spotted hand patted my own. "Don't worry about her none," an old man said. He tugged at the terrier's leash. "You keep away from them flowers," he commanded. And turning to me he added, "She can't stand dogs or cats, or kids for that matter. She hated the old lady," he nodded toward the hearse as it made its quiet retreat down the street under the arching maples. "Tried to get the city to make her clean up her yard, complained that the seeds blew across into her garden, messed up her pretty arrangements. And the number of times she had the Humane Society here looking out for them cats!" His cackle degenerated into a shaky cough. After some fumbling, he found a shred of tissue which he used for both his nose and his eyes. "'Scuse me," he said. "But I was kind of fond of the old witch."

"Who?"

"Mother Baker." He nodded at the little house across the street. "That's what we all called her, anyways. Not to her face, mind. She used to tell fortunes in the old days, reading tea leaves. Didn't always hear what you wanted neither, but she was right more times than not. Old as the devil she was. Older'n me, anyways, and I won't see seventy again. Guess how old I am, young lady. Go ahead — guess."

"I don't know. Seventy-two?"

That got him laughing again. "Eighty," he hooted. "Eighty years old and lived here all my life. Born in that house right there" — he pointed to an immaculate Victorian house on the corner, complete with tower and gingerbread fretwork — "and I'm going to die there, too. Got my granddaughter living with me now. Her and her kids. She needs a place to live and I need the company. Whereabouts do you live, eh? Don't recall seeing you round about, and I know everybody on this street."

Before I could answer him, another stir swept through the crowd as a small van came up to the curb. A policeman hurried over to talk to the driver. The back opened and a young woman climbed down, carrying two pet carriers and a long pole with a loop of rope at its end.

"They're going to catch the cats," the old man said. "I gotta watch this."

He tugged his dog back across the street and took up a station under one of the big maples that lined the sidewalk. I followed.

The police car pulled out of the drive and passed us. Its driver was intent on weaving a safe path through the crowd; her passenger was scribbling in a notebook with one hand while talking into a radio mike he held in the other. On the street, a uniformed officer was talking to various onlookers, taking notes as they answered his questions. The boys rode their bikes back and forth, craning their necks to peer inside the house through the open door.

An unholy screech erupted from inside. One of the men I'd noticed earlier stumbled out on to the porch, blood dripping from a hand he held so that it wouldn't stain his pale linen suit. "Damned cats," he snarled. "I hate cats."

"Take it easy, Joe." The second, younger man joined him. He was trying not to smile, but I could see that he privately enjoyed the other's distress. "It's just a little scratch."

"Did you see the one that bit me? Big as a lion it was."

"Scared of a little pussy, are you?"

"I didn't see you trying to catch it." Joe pulled a starched handkerchief from his vest pocket and wrapped it around his palm. "Probably has rabies," he grumbled. "I'll have to get those shots. Have you got any idea how bad those shots are? I heard they give you about forty of them, right in the belly. I hate needles."

"You think Workmen's Compensation will cover this? Cat scratch in the line of duty?" the other man ribbed him.

Joe muttered another curse, turning his back on his partner to survey the street. I didn't look away quickly enough. We stared at each other for a long moment. Without dropping his eyes, Joe whispered something to the younger man. He too looked at me. I decided it was time to leave.

The cat catchers came out, staggering with the weight of two boxes each, boxes that snarled and shook as the cats inside fought to escape. They slid them into the van and brought out four more empty cases. The woman sighed heavily before turning back to the house.

"They'll be bringing them out for hours." My old friend was back beside me again. He was carrying the little dog, which had become bored with all the action and fallen asleep.

"She had a lot of cats?"

"You bet. It was all the grocery ever delivered, cat food and milk."

"What about her? What did she eat?"

"Regular food, I guess. She walked down to the corner every other day of the week, 'cept Sunday, rain or shine, pulling that little bundle buggy of hers. It was company for her, going to the store."

"But the cat food got delivered?"

"Bags of it, yeah." He nodded. "Every stray for miles around knew to come to Mother Baker's come October. Most of 'em had kittens and most of the little ones stayed. They just burst out of that house in the evening. Mrs. Robinson," and he nodded toward the home of the first woman I'd approached, "she used to complain all the time. But the old lady was clever. She had them all named and had the vet come and give them their shots. She even had the papers to prove it. Fifty cats she had. I know — the vet told me when she came to see Winny here, the last time Winny ate something he shouldn't." He rubbed his cheek against the dog's head. Its tail thumped against his chest, but its eyes stayed closed. "Garbage mouths, dogs are! You have to love them, though. Not like cats. Can't say I like them either, but they were company to the old woman. Only family she had, I'd say. Look," and he nodded to the other house. "Here she comes."

Mrs. Robinson stalked down her sidewalk and right across the street to the van. She waited for the next load of cats to be dumped inside. "They killed her, didn't they?" she demanded. "Those cats ganged up on her, right? She fell and couldn't feed them, right? They ate her. I told you and told you they were dangerous. I knew something like this would happen, I just knew." Her voice cracked.

The uniformed officer had finished speaking to the last of the group on the far sidewalk, and waved them off to their homes. He hurried across to the driveway, but the scratched detective beat him to her. He put his hand on her arm and drew her away from the van. The two Humane Society officers grinned at each other. One drew circles in the air around his ear. The other shrugged and picked up two more empty cases.

"Guilt," the old man hissed.

"What?" I was trying to hear what Joe was telling the woman, but they were too far off, their voices lowered in intimate whispers.

"Guilt," he repeated. "She always said she wished the old lady would die and take her cats with her. She can't stand it now that it's happened."

"The cats really didn't eat her?" I shuddered at the vision.

"No. Mrs. Robinson watches too much TV. You know, those American crime shows, rescue squads, whatever. Bunch of baloney, if you ask me. Pets wouldn't do such a thing. Not 'less they were really starving, and it couldn't be more'n a day since the old lady died."

"What happened to her?"

He shook his head. "Ah, it's a sad story, sad indeed. Mr. Iannou was telling me." He nodded toward the other old man who was now arguing with Mrs. Robinson and the cop. "He found her, you know. Lives next door, has lived there fifty years, and I daresay she's never said more'n two words at a stretch to him. 'Good day' — you know. Or 'Fine evening.' But he kept an eye out for her, specially once that woman moved in and started on about the cats. Anyways, he realized he hadn't seen her for two days. Regular as clockwork she was, letting the cats in and out, once in the morning, once in the evening. And today was her church morning. She never missed a morning service, not even in winter. But today, nothing. So he knocks on the door and all he hears is them cats squalling. So he calls the cops."

Mrs. Robinson stamped past us back to her house. She was muttering, but I couldn't quite hear what she said. I didn't want to hear it.

"And?" I prompted the old fellow.

"And they break down the door. And they find her, at the

bottom of the stairs. Fell she had, and died. Funny, though."

"What?"

"Them stairs. Been years since those windows on the top floor been boarded up. Can't imagine what she'd been doing going up there. Even I have some trouble with stairs these days. Moved my bed down to the dining room. Granddaughter says it's a good thing I put in that first floor toilet when Martha took ill. Martha was my wife. Fifty-two years together we had. Fifty-two wonderful years. Are you married?"

"Granddad, what are you doing?" A young woman thrust herself in between me and the old man. In spite of her designer jeans and tailored cotton shirt, she was disheveled, almost frumpy. "It's not just the boys I have to watch, but you too, is it?" she whined. "I go to lie down for just five minutes, and off you go. I've been looking all over the house. I should have realized you'd be out here with all the ghouls." She sniffed angrily and glared at me. "Who are you? What do you want with my grandfather?"

"We were just talking," I said.

"That's no way to be speaking to a stranger, a lady at that," the old man grumbled. "Didn't your mother teach you better manners, girl?"

"Spare me the lecture." She tugged at his arm. "And put that damn dog down. You'll strain your back carrying him around."

"He don't weigh hardly anything," the old man protested. He sighed, then did as she said.

"You're coming home with me this minute. I bet you forgot your pills again, too, didn't you? You know you're supposed to take them at exactly three p.m., and it's half-past already. You're worse than the boys. A grown man you are, you ought to know better."

"Don't worry, girl, I'll be all right this once. I had to say good-bye to Mrs. Baker now, didn't I? She's the last of the old ones to go. 'Cept me, of course, and with you looking out for me, I got no worries about that happening too soon, eh?" He chuckled, and gently patted her shoulder.

She flushed. "Oh, you." She pushed his hand away and then clutched it. "You'll be the death of me, you know."

"Come on, then, let's go take those pills. See what those

scallywags of yours are up to."

"Oh my god, the boys." She dropped his hand and ran off, her sandals slapping the pavement.

"Your granddaughter?" I asked.

"She loves me." The old man shook his head. "Don't know why, but there it is. I let her boss me round some, but don't take much notice of her tone. She can't help it. She had bad luck with that man of hers, left her with two little ones and a third on the way. The baby's two now, sweet little thing. She needed a home and I had that big old place, too big for me to keep up myself after the wife died. Family should stick together, eh? Well, I best be going before she's out here after me with a frying pan." He chuckled. "Got a temper that one has, just like her grandma. Come on then, Winston, old boy. Time to go home. Good-day."

I was ready to leave as well. I turned to find my way blocked by the plainclothes officer with the scratched palm.

"Excuse me." He was very polite. "May I have a word with you, ma'am?"

It was too late to pretend to be uninvolved, a passerby. Once again, my curiosity, like a cat's, had caught me.

TWO

The cop smiled and flipped his badge. "I'm Detective Joe Gianelli. And you are?"

"Rosalie Cairns," I said. "What happened in there?"

"You live around here?" he asked.

"I hate people who answer questions with questions," I retorted.

"It's my job," he shrugged. "Let's get the preliminaries over with, okay?"

I sighed and gave him the address, not just of my apartment here in the city, but of my house in the town where my husband lives and has his business.

"You're separated?" He looked me up and down. From the way his eyes shifted from belligerence to attentive friendliness, I realized he must like what he saw. I wasn't wearing my usual graduate school uniform of jeans and bulky sweater, but had dressed up for tea in my one good outfit: burgundy suede jacket over a white silk blouse and black linen slacks. He and I were about the same age, in our early forties, but he used dye to keep his thinning hair black while I ignore the gray that streaks through the mass of curls I still wear long and loose in spite of the aggravation it causes. I took up swimming this past year, an hour a day in the university pool. Trying to stuff all that hair into a bathing cap almost ruins the pleasure of competing against myself for more and more laps.

"No, not separated." I answered curtly.

"Divorced, then?"

"No."

"You work here? You commute?"

"It's too far to commute. That's why I have a place here. I'm in graduate school at York." I searched in my bag for my spectacle case and switched from the oversize dark prescription lenses to my wire frames. The sudden brightness made me blink.

"What does he do? Your husband?"

"He's a carpenter/contractor, renovates old houses, that kind of thing. He's just started his company and can't leave the business. I go home most weekends."

"Who takes care of the kids? I assume you have kids."

"I thought cops didn't make assumptions," I snapped. "And no, we have no kids."

"So you're all on your own here."

My hand itched to slap the smirk from his face. I counted to ten — slowly. Losing my temper would only worsen matters. I took a deep breath and spoke clearly and slowly, as if to a child: "I'm working. I'm in the library most days, and most nights too, for that matter. I don't have much time for socializing. It seemed like a good idea when I decided to come back to school, to take an apartment here until my course work is done. As soon as this academic year is over, I'll be moving home."

I could hardly wait for the school year to end. Once my oral exams were over, I would be free to research and write my thesis, and I could do that in my own study in my own house. When I had first come to the city, I'd rented a tiny bachelor apartment on the twenty-fourth floor of a highrise, in a development in the suburbs near York University. The windows wouldn't open and the elevator always stopped at every single floor going up or down, although no one seemed to be waiting for it. The walk to classes along Keele Street past strip plazas and car dealerships was a misery of slush, biting winds, and exhaust fumes. Living downtown meant I had a long transit ride out to campus, but I was close to the Robarts Library for my research. Everything I needed was within walking distance: Kensington Market for food, Chinatown for inexpensive but interesting meals out, bookstores, movie theatres, the

University of Toronto campus with its sports complex and myriad cultural activities. Sometimes, I felt like an undergraduate again, twenty years old and carefree; and, far too often, lonely.

I missed my dog, Sadie, and our walks along the river close to our house. I missed Will. Our time together was always too short, a fever of talk and love-making. There was always so much to do: work on the house, work on my courses, seeing friends, shopping and laundry. I looked back almost with nostalgia on those long, slow days of underemployment, when I worked part-time at a bookstore. It was easy to forget how bored I'd been then.

Gianelli looked down at his notebook. "This street's not exactly in your neighbourhood," he said. "Are you visiting someone around here?" He managed to make his question sound suggestive.

"I was on my way to my aunt's. She'd invited me to tea."

"And she lives?"

"Right behind you."

He swivelled and stared at the little house as if he'd never seen it before. The animal control officers slammed the van door on the final load of cats. They waved to Gianelli before driving away. He grimaced.

"Who's this?" It was the man who had ribbed Gianelli about the cat scratch. He was younger than either of us, a black giant in a rumpled blue suit. His shoulders strained at the polyester fabric. From the way he balanced on the balls of his feet, I could tell he was one of those guys who worked on his muscles at a gym. A cop with a "Terminator" complex: what a cliché. His body was taut and sculptured now, but I shuddered inwardly to think how he would appear in thirty years when age took its revenge.

"Detective Wilson," he shook my hand in a vise grip.

"You're partners?" I asked.

"Not exactly," he laughed. "We work out of the same division. Happened to be on our way to lunch when the call came in and he wanted to check it out. I'd leave it up to the constables, but ... my friend here is looking for a Big Case, get his name in the papers. Hey, Gianelli, you started frothing yet?"

"Lay off," Gianelli growled. "This is a relative."

"Of the old lady?" Wilson's smile hardened. "How could

you let her live like that? Die like that? You been to see her lately? Like in the last decade or so? You should be ashamed."

"I've never even met her. I didn't even know I had an aunt until she wrote me."

"You got the letter with you?" Gianelli ignored the younger man and held out his hand to me.

I handed him the envelope. He compared the address on it with the one I'd given him and eased the letter out with care. He held it at arm's length, squinting as he read the short message. He should have been wearing the bifocals I glimpsed in his breast pocket.

Wilson grabbed the letter away from him. "Can't you read any faster? Where're your glasses? *Dear Mrs. Cairns* — that's you, I presume?"

I nodded. Gianelli pulled a silver cigarette case out from an inside pocket. He tapped it open and offered it to me. I shook my head. He chose a filter tip and made a show of lighting it with a gold lighter. The sun winked on the diamond in his pinky ring. He was exceedingly well dressed for duty.

Wilson continued to read: "*I understand that you are the only daughter of my nephew, George Cook. It would please an old woman greatly if you were to forgive the neglect of the past, and come to visit me for tea next Wednesday, at three p.m., at the address above. You may find it in your interest to attend. I look forward to meeting you. I am, your dear Aunt, Beatrice Baker.* Will you listen to that? Talk about formal."

"What's this about past neglect?" Gianelli demanded.

"I told you I never met her. My father left when I was just a baby, and my mother never talked about his family. I just assumed he hadn't any, but was an only child like me. Only child of an only child — it was something special we shared. That I thought we shared."

"You think she was going to give you something? Take you back in the bosom of the family?"

"I didn't want anything from her. I wasn't going to come at all at first, but I was curious. I might have cousins. She might have pictures of my father and my grandparents." I blinked away sudden tears. "I just wanted to meet her. To see where I came from. Is that so hard to understand?"

Wilson folded the letter and put it back in the envelope. He hesitated before handing it back to me. I put it in my bag — so much for family.

"You were pretty cosy with that old fellow with the dog," Gianelli said. "You been around already? Checking out the place maybe?"

"I'd never seen him before today. He just wanted to talk to someone. You know how old people like to talk."

"Yeah." He blew a long stream of thin smoke, a dragon tired of chewing up the little folk. "You're not planning on leaving town, are you?"

"Give her a break, Joe," Wilson smiled at me. "We may want to talk to you again — after we speak to Mrs. Baker's lawyer."

"Could I look inside?" I asked. I didn't want to have come all this way for nothing. It was not just the time wasted on the long subway and streetcar rides, but the whole journey I'd gone through in the week since receiving the letter. I had struggled with the memories of my mother and the painful hate she had insisted on in every discussion of my father and his family. "They'll never get their hands on you," she would say. "They're rotten, every last one of them."

"Who?" I'd ask, when I still asked her questions about them. "Do I have an Oma and Opa like Annie does?" Annie was my best friend, daughter of the large and boisterous family who shared our duplex. There were constant streams of relatives coming and going downstairs. I was informally adopted into the tribe, but there were days when I was left behind: when the families gathered for a wedding or a christening at some uncle's distant house. There wasn't room in any of their cars then for me. My mother refused to talk about my father or any of the Cooks. "They're dead to us," she said, when I pressed her too hard with my queries. "They never wanted either of us when you were born. We don't need them. We've got each other and that's all we'll ever want." And that was all she'd say.

I sighed, and shook off the memories. I'd decided at long last to come here, and I had come too late.

Gianelli and Wilson exchanged glances heavy with some kind of warning I couldn't interpret.

"Maybe you can go in later," Gianelli muttered. "Maybe tomorrow if the lawyer agrees."

"But it's a long way," I pleaded. "And I haven't got a car.

Would it hurt for me just to look around a bit? See her things? There might be pictures of her family. My family, I mean. I won't take anything, and you can come in with me. Please?"

"Sorry." Wilson scuffed at a crack in the sidewalk. "We can't let anyone in until the coroner's finished with the post mortem. Regulations."

"Coroner?" I was confused. "I thought she died of a fall."

"Not exactly." Gianelli dropped his cigarette butt and rubbed it out viciously with the toe of one shoe. I couldn't help noticing his footwear: blood-red leather oxfords. Nice. He continued. "It looks like she ran into something. Or something ran into her."

"The cats, you mean?"

"A bit bigger than that."

"Are you talking about a burglary?"

"No." He rubbed his hand over his skull, careful not to rearrange his hair. "I'm talking about murder."

"Murder?" I leaned back heavily against the maple tree, thankful for the solidity of its rough trunk. I was suddenly very tired. I stifled a yawn. My eyes burned. "I thought it was routine, you being here."

"Let's sit a minute." Wilson cupped my left elbow in his big hand. He tugged gently; I let him lead me to the porch. He made a show of pulling out from his pants pocket a handkerchief as big as a scarf which he spread on the top step before gently pressing me to sit.

Gianelli sauntered up. He stood looking up at us, one foot on the bottom of the four wooden steps, both hands deep in his pants pockets. "You okay?"

I nodded. "It's a shock. I mean, I was just getting used to the idea of having an aunt, and now she's dead. Maybe murdered." I shook my head. "Why me?" My voice rose in a wail of complaint.

The officers exchanged glances. Before they could comment, however, a commotion on the street distracted them.

A long black limousine nosed its way through the thinning crowd of neighbours. It pulled into the driveway, stopped, the engine purring no louder than one of the recently departed cats. The driver didn't bother looking our way when he got out, but bent to open the back door. He wasn't exactly wearing a uniform, but the trim cut of his gray overcoat and his formal stance as he gave an arm to the elderly gentleman who was struggling to stand, clearly showed him to be a chauffeur. I'd never met a real chauffeur before. I'd never met anyone who had the means or the need to have one.

The old man steadied himself, his weight borne by a black knobbed stick with a rubber tip and elaborately carved silver handle. He looked rich and cold, the black fur collar of his long cashmere coat pulled high around his face which was small and white under the brim of a lamb's wool cossack hat. He shook off his servant's helping hand and hobbled toward us. The driver got back into the car, ignoring the younger man who clambered out of the back seat and quickly overtook his senior. The old man also ignored him, concentrating instead on the cracked sidewalk. We could hear the faint whistling of his breath as he made his way towards us.

The younger man reached the stairs first. "What's going on here?" he demanded. His voice was high and thin, the intonation suggestive of a British accent. Or of a Canadian accent which was trying to sound British.

Before any of us could answer, the old man spoke directly to me. "You must be George Cook's daughter?"

I nodded yes.

"And these gentlemen?"

Gianelli introduced himself and Wilson.

"Detectives!" the younger man exclaimed. He looked up at the house as he asked, "Mrs. Baker?"

"I'm sorry," Gianelli replied. "She was found this morning."

"Any sudden unexplained death has to be checked out," Wilson added.

"Surely it wasn't unexpected," the old man said. He swayed on his cane. A small clear droplet hung from the end of his nose, stretched, fell on the high collar. His companion reached out to take his arm, but the old fellow shrugged him off. "Beatrice was ninety-three years old. Her time had come. But murder! I doubt that. She had no enemies."

"She was found at the bottom of the stairs. With a broken neck," Gianelli said.

"Accident then."

"I tend to agree..." Wilson began.

Gianelli interrupted him. "You're the lawyer? Dufferin Ross?"

"That's right." The old man held out a trembling hand which Gianelli gently shook. "How do you know my name?"

"She had your card taped to the wall beside her phone. We called your office ..."

"We were on our way anyway."

"Is that what that call on the car phone was about?" The younger man's voice rose even higher. "Why didn't you tell me?"

"You were too engrossed in the stock market reports," the old man retorted. I caught the glint in his eye and realized he must have enjoyed not just keeping this small secret from his companion, but also the other's obvious dismay at finding the police at their client's home.

Gianelli interrupted their tiff. "And your name, sir?"

"Roger Markham. Of Ross, Armour and Markham. Mrs. Baker is one of my uncle's oldest clients."

"Friend, boy," the old man grunted. "Some of us are friends with our clients. We can see beyond the bills."

Markham flushed, but continued. "We had an appointment with Mrs. Baker today. To see her great-niece. Putative great-niece," he added. "I told him I didn't like this idea from the beginning; that there'd be trouble. And I was right."

The old man wasn't listening. His eyes never left my face, eyes of a very pale blue, almost colourless beneath the thick white wings of his brows. His skin was stretched tight over the bones, the only wrinkles in nests at the corners of his eyes and in deep grooves that ran from his sharp nose down to the edge of his lips. Small red patches glowed on his cheeks; his lips were pale and, as I watched him, the small pink tip of his tongue ran out and around them. I looked away.

"So, you know this woman?" Gianelli asked.

"Knew her father. Feckless boy. Knew them all. Not her, though. Mother took her away. Let's take a look at you, then. Come down here, where I can see you properly."

I stood up reluctantly and came down the stairs. Markham had to step into the grass to make room for me on the pavement beside his uncle. He grimaced as he stepped in something soft, and began to wipe the sole of his shoe over and over on the edge of the concrete path. The rasp irritated the old man. He spoke over one shoulder.

"Why don't you wait in the car, my boy? You didn't have to come with me. I can still do business on my own."

"It's all right, Uncle. I don't mind waiting."

The old man shrugged. Before I could back away, he grabbed my chin with one hand, cold and bony as a claw, and turned my head from one side to the other.

"You have your grandmother's eyes," he said. He dropped his hand to join the other on the top of the cane.

I shivered. I could feel the faint crescent dents of his finger-nails in the skin of my cheeks.

"My mother didn't take me away," I said to him. "My father left us."

"That's what she told you, is it?"

"That's what happened."

He shook his head and was about to speak again when Gianelli repeated his question: "Is this Mrs. Baker's niece?"

"Great-niece," Mr. Ross corrected. "Beatrice's brother's granddaughter."

"You knew she was coming to visit her here?"

"I suggested we meet in my office, but Beatrice refused to come downtown. She didn't like the traffic and she didn't want to leave her cats. Filthy things," the old man sniffed. He looked narrowly at the house. "They still in there?"

"The Humane Society took them away," Wilson said.

"Good. Then what are we standing out here in the cold for? Let's go in."

THREE

Mr. Ross used his cane to brush the two policemen aside and hauled himself up the stairs. I followed, with Markham, Gianelli and Wilson close behind.

"We should keep out until the coroner is satisfied," Wilson objected as Mr. Ross pushed the front door open.

"Nothing to find," the old man grunted. "Accident. Old age. Waste of time looking for anything else. Comes to all of us sooner or later."

"Now, Uncle," Markham soothed. "Don't get yourself upset. Maybe we should call this meeting off and get together another day."

"We have business here," Mr. Ross nodded at me. "I'll miss Beatrice, true enough. Last of a breed, she was, a real lady. Haven't seen much of her since my dear Anne passed away." He sniffed. "And since you young fellows have taken over the office. Retirement, they call it," he said to Gianelli. He made the sound that comic books rendered as "hmmph." I'd never believed real people did that.

"I'm cold," he continued. "Beatrice would be mortified to think we were all standing out here on the street, making a spectacle of ourselves for the neighbours. She would want us to come in."

Mr. Ross knew where to go in the house, turning to the right in the dark hall that was a minefield of litter boxes and bowls. He pushed aside a floor-length velvet curtain which rattled along a brass rod to reveal a room as dusty and still as a museum display. Lace curtains kept out most of whatever light could penetrate the grimy windows that were further darkened by alternating panes of dull red and green leaded glass. After a moment's fumbling he flicked a switch which turned on a pale yellow globe that hung from the centre of an elaborately plastered ceiling now webbed with a million fine cracks. He stumped across to an oversized wing chair upholstered in red corduroy. When he sat, a fine cloud of dust rose around him. He sneezed.

Besides that chair, the room was stuffed with a matching sofa, two more armchairs, and a footstool; a wooden rocker covered with a frayed quilt; an elaborately carved upright piano; a tall bookshelf filled with books whose spines were so faded their titles were impossible to read; and a bow-fronted china cabinet. Every surface bore a load of knick-knacks: china figurines, gold-rimmed tea cups on lace doilies, painted bowls of dried flowers and even a lithe creature, mink or marten, mounted on a piece of driftwood and glaring at us with its glass eyes. On a black table pushed against one wall was a crowd of picture frames. I headed straight for it.

"Just a minute," Wilson said. "You're not to touch anything."

The three men pushed into the room, Markham edging in front of the two cops. He grabbed my arm. I pulled away from him and in doing so backed into the table. The frames fell like a set of dominoes, one after the other, knocking pictures flat. I grabbed a silver oval disc as it slipped over the edge.

"My goodness," Mr. Ross exclaimed. "Be careful, Roger. Come and sit down, Mrs. Cairns. That is your name now, isn't it?"

He pointed with his stick at the sofa. I obeyed, still clutching the photo in my hands. Markham muttered an apology and stood back, almost but not quite leaning against the wall. Gianelli looked at one of the armchairs for a moment, as if tempted to sit, but the dust and the layer of cat hairs that covered it discouraged him. Wilson didn't mind. He plunked down so heavily on the other end of the sofa that I distinctly heard a spring pop.

Mr. Ross sat on the edge of the huge chair, his hands folded on top of the cane, his chin nearly resting on them. He had taken off his hat and placed it on the floor where it rested, like a contented cat curled by his feet.

Gianelli was determined to take control of the interview. "You claim that this woman is a relative of the deceased?" he asked the old lawyer again.

"Of course, young man. I helped Beatrice locate her. There's not much of the family left and she felt badly about what had happened. She wanted to make amends."

"What did happen?" Wilson asked.

"It was long ago," the old man waved a hand. "Nothing to do with this. An old story."

"I'd like to know," I said.

"The point is," Markham added, "that she will now inherit considerable property."

"What?" I said at the same moment that Gianelli asked, "This house?"

Mr. Ross shook his head. "No, no. Her grandfather's summer home. Did your mother never tell you about the Cooks?" he said to me.

I shook my head, staring down at the yellowed photograph in my hand. Posed in front of a draped curtain and Grecian urn were two children, the boy dressed in a sailor suit with knee pants and a white cap, the girl in a lacy dress that reached to her ankles.

"Who are they?" I asked, handing the picture to Mr. Ross.

He studied it, holding it out at arm's length. "That would be your grandfather and your great-aunt Beatrice when they were children. This must be in the library of the Cook house over on Brunswick Avenue. It's gone now."

"Excuse me," Gianelli broke in. "But what property are you talking about? That she inherits?" He jerked his thumb at me.

"The original Cook claim: one hundred acres of farm land up north. Beatrice wanted Mrs. Cairns to have it. It's rightfully hers after all, has been for years."

"That's not exactly true," Markham interrupted.

Mr. Ross turned on him. "You, boy, you don't know the half of it. There's what's legal and there's what's right. Beatrice wanted to do what's right and I, as her lawyer and the executor of the estate, am going to carry out her wishes."

"Other people have interests here," Markham objected.

"Other people have no business in what doesn't concern them," the old man snapped. "Your job is to manage accounts, not make decisions about my clients. Not that you've left me that many. But Beatrice trusted me, and I made sure her will was up-to-date and binding. There's no question of contest. No question at all."

"Perhaps you'll explain what you're talking about?" Gianelli asked.

"We'll begin at the beginning," the old man leaned back in the chair, his voice already slipping into the slight singsong of the raconteur.

Wilson sighed. He patted a pocket as if looking for cigarettes. He shook his head and began to pick idly at a loose hair on the arm of the sofa. He must have just quit smoking. He had that yearning look.

Mr. Ross launched into his story. "The Cooks came over from Belfast in the middle of the last century and took up land in Haliburton. One hundred acres of rock and swamp on the shore of a big lake they named for themselves. The oldest boy left for the city, went into the undertaking business, while the daughter's husband, a McDonnel, tried to keep the farm going. There were two younger boys, but they went out west and lost touch with the others."

"So there are McDonnel cousins and other Cooks as well?" I asked.

He ignored my interruption. "The McDonnels fell on hard times while George Cook prospered, as did his son. He paid the taxes while the McDonnels worked the land. Then your grandfather decided to give his new wife a summer home. This was about 1925 or '26, something in there. He claimed the lake property back."

"What about the McDonnels? Wasn't the place theirs?"

The old lawyer shrugged. "Those who pay the taxes own the land. And remember, George had title. The McDonnels threatened to sue, but they didn't have a leg to stand on. One of them still lives up there somewhere, I believe. He'd be an old man by now."

Wilson looked at his watch. "What's this got to do with Mrs.

Cairns and the old lady?"

"Ah well," Mr. Ross said. "It all comes down to family in the end, who belongs, who doesn't. George, her grandfather," he jabbed his thumb at me, "hated his son's English wife, specially after she left him. He almost wrote little Rosalie out of his will. But she was family, and, after young George died, she was the last of the Cooks. So he wanted her to have the property in the end."

"When?" I asked. "When did he die?"

"In 1961."

"Then why did no one contact me until now?"

"Let me finish," Mr. Ross commanded. "Your grandfather hated your mother." He held up his hand to quiet my objections. "Even after she left young George and wouldn't take any maintenance from him. Old George couldn't forgive her."

"For leaving her husband? But he beat her," I protested. I squeezed my eyes shut. I would not allow myself to cry in front of these men.

"That's what she said, but I never saw any bruises. He said he slapped her once, when she insisted on going out instead of taking care of you. Your grandmother never believed he would hurt any woman, not on purpose, not without being provoked. She said your mother never got over the war, the rationing and misery. That she married your father to get out of England and then wouldn't settle down to be a proper wife and mother."

"She was a wonderful mother," I protested. "She worked really hard for both of us."

"That's as may be," Mr. Ross said. "Fact is, she left young George and took you with her, wouldn't let your grandparents see you. I tried to help. I even got her a job with a friend of mine..."

"Mr. McIntosh? You knew Mr. McIntosh?" I broke in. My mother's employer had been like an elderly uncle to me. On my rare visits to the office, he always spoke to me about school and friends while offering a choice of biscuits from the tin he kept on his desk. And at Christmas there was always a wrapped present under the tree for me from him.

"When I saw how determined she was, I figured it was best to leave her where we could keep tabs on her. It was a good job she had there; she worked herself up from receptionist to secretary.

She made me promise not to tell the family where you lived. She said that if George ever tried to contact her, she'd take you and disappear. He asked me often enough, but I never told."

"He never visited us." I remembered my old sorrow, my constant questions when I first went to school and discovered that other children lived with two parents. I wanted a Daddy desperately. I remember once running home in tears, asking my mother what was a bastard and why was being one so bad? She told me that I did have a father and that he was dead. After that, I had a certain cachet at school, being an orphan. I told the other kids that my father had been a fighter pilot and killed in the war. The fact that I was born six years after the war ended was never mentioned.

"For the first two years he kept asking me where you were," Mr. Ross said. "That man was just eaten with remorse. There was never proof that he ever lifted a hand against your mother. Except that one slap he owned up to. It was her word against his."

"And she was just a war bride, with no family."

He bowed his head. "I did what I could."

"What about me?" I asked. "Didn't my grandparents ever try to see me?"

"Oh yes. After young George passed away, they tried to persuade your mother to let them adopt you, send you to a good school, give you your proper place in life. They even suggested you both come to live with them. They offered to give your mother rooms in the carriage house. Your mother would have nothing to do with them."

"Good for her. How dare they treat her like a servant."

Mr. Ross shrugged. "They were old-fashioned folk. Doesn't matter now."

"What about this will?" Gianelli interrupted. "You want to get around to it, please?"

"Well, George couldn't stand the thought of Maisie getting her hands on the property. He knew he wouldn't survive another heart attack and the girl was only ten years old. So he left it to Beatrice. He asked her to give it to Rosalie when her mother died."

"But she didn't," I exclaimed. "I never heard from her until last week."

"Thing is," said Mr. Ross, "Beatrice loved that cottage. She couldn't bear to give it up. Legally it was hers to do with what she wanted. She knew you'd never made any effort to contact the family..."

"My mother always told me that my father was an orphan," I protested.

"Beatrice needed an excuse for hanging on. She kept saying the time wasn't right to tell you. But last summer she was too frail to go up to the lake. She wanted to make amends. I told her it was about time."

"I didn't expect anything like this," I said. "I just wanted to meet her to find out about my father's family."

"So you didn't know you were an heir," Gianelli said. He had been taking notes in a small leather book. He turned to the lawyer. "Who else benefits?"

"Really, officer," Markham interrupted. "This isn't the time or place to discuss motive, is it? You don't even know for sure that her death wasn't accidental. An old lady like that, steep stairs — aren't you assuming a crime that doesn't exist?"

"Did you know about the property?"

"It doesn't have anything to do with me," Markham protested. "I've been administering the estate for my uncle. With his advice. That's all."

"What's the land worth?" Wilson asked.

"A lot of money. One hundred acres of prime cottage country with one thousand feet of pristine shoreline." Markham's voice was wistful. "Developers have been after it for years."

"You know the conditions," Mr. Ross said. He turned to me, "Your grandfather had a special request for Beatrice to pass on to you. If you don't want to keep it, the property is to go to the province for a bird sanctuary. He didn't want to see the land divided up."

"It's not written in the will itself," Markham objected. "It's just a letter of intent. Ms. Cairns can do what she wants once she has the deed."

"Not everyone is mercenary," the old man's voice dripped acid.

Markham flushed.

"This is all very interesting," Gianelli said. "But you haven't answered my question: who else stands to gain?"

"If the old lady was murdered," Markham said, "*she's* got a pretty good motive."

"That's enough, Roger." The old man struggled to his feet. "I'm tired. I want to go home."

"And the cottage?" Wilson asked.

"It's yours, my dear," Ross took my hand and bowed slightly. "I will make arrangements for the papers to be sent to you. May you long enjoy it."

"Just a minute," Gianelli said. "We have an investigation going on here."

Ross was already at the door. He turned and frowned at the two policemen. "Waste of time, I said. She was old, she fell. It's simple."

"A neighbour said the upstairs was blocked off," Gianelli objected. "She had no reason to go up there."

"Maybe she was looking for something to show Mrs. Cairns. A keepsake from her brother, perhaps. Who's to know? Old folk do strange things at times." He chuckled. "Even me. Let the dead rest. There's no good in stirring up old bones. The only secret in this house was the ownership of a parcel of land in the wilds. And the only ones who knew the true story of that were Beatrice and I. Mrs. Cairns is innocent. It's sad, though, my dear, that you never did meet your aunt. A real lady, she was. A real lady." He pushed aside the curtain and went out.

"He may say so, but it's not the last you'll be hearing from the firm," Markham said. "There are a few questions yet to be answered." He followed his uncle.

"Well," Wilson stood up and brushed off his pants. Cat hair fell in a fine shower to the rug. "Let's get out of here."

"Shouldn't you have made them answer your questions?" I asked Gianelli. "Found out who else does benefit? Who else had opportunity? How could you just let them go like that?"

"You read a lot of detective stories?"

I blushed. "My thesis is on women detective novelists."

"It would be." Gianelli winked at his partner. "It's one of the interrogation techniques we've perfected. We let everyone else do the talking, and see what comes out. If all the suspects keep blabbing, someone's going to confess."

"Easy business, this is," Wilson yawned. "No glamour. Just sit around listening to a lot of hot air and take notes. Make connections. Regular Nero Wolfes, we are."

"Yeah," Gianelli said. He stretched. "Time enough to get down to a real investigation after we hear from the coroner."

"I wish you wouldn't be dreaming up work," Wilson complained. "Always wanting to turn a simple accident into a major murder case. It looks pretty straightforward to me, and I've been to a lot more murder scenes than you have."

"She's one of the names on my list..." Gianelli began. His glance slid toward me and he stopped.

"What list?" I prompted.

He shook his head. "A case I'm working on. Not murder."

"A cop I know at home always claims coincidence and accident when he means murder."

"What cop is that?"

"His name's Constable Finlay."

"He's a friend of yours?"

"Not exactly." I shrugged. "I've met him a few times. It's a small town."

Wilson sighed dramatically. "I'm starving, and we still haven't made it to lunch. This seems to me pretty cut-and-dried. Let's get going, okay? We're neither of us Kojak. Even if one of us is a little thin on top."

"Give me a break," Gianelli snorted, but couldn't help smoothing one hand over the strands of hair combed across his scalp. "Good day, ma'am," he nodded to me. He cocked his finger at Wilson. "You, I'll see outside."

The front door slammed behind him.

Wilson grinned. "Would you like a ride home?" he asked me.

"I'll take the bus." I went over to the table and began to pick up photographs, staring at the faces who smiled back at me. This one was of a girl who must be my age now. In the picture she was a teenager in a purple paisley shirt dress with long straight hair almost to her waist. She wore white stockings and purple shoes with those big clunky heels that Elton John made so popular. She was standing on the porch of this house. It was freshly painted and the cedars that now overshadowed the roof were small trimmed bushes on each side of the steps. She held a cat in her arms.

"Let's go, then." He took the picture and replaced it on the table. One hand on my elbow, he steered me out the door.

Gianelli was standing on the front porch. He locked the door behind us, and put the key in his pocket. "I've got your address," he reminded me. "We'll be in touch if we need to talk to you again."

The two men sauntered across the lawn. I heard Wilson laugh again as they reached their car and Gianelli's explosive curse. I wondered if the younger man was ribbing him this time about his hair or about the cats.

I pulled my jacket tight against the small wind that had sprung up with the setting of the sun. I was now a person of property, though still without family. Shadows lay thickly on the street under streetlights that glowed with faint jaundiced light. More cars were parked along both sides of the street. In many houses the curtains had already been drawn and lamps lit. I could hear quite clearly the grumble of traffic on Queen Street and the shriek of a streetcar's tired brakes. Far off, a siren whooped. Behind me, the house seemed to hunch itself over its secrets, nursing its empty rooms as a cat worries a flea bite. I shivered. Somewhere nearby a door slammed and the Doberman began to bark, an anxious menace. It was time to go home.

Although the streetcar was packed, I was surprised to see a seat empty except for a bulging green garbage bag. I edged towards it. The other half was occupied by a woman dressed in a tattered gray tweed overcoat, a red polka dot scarf tied so tightly around her head that no hair showed at all. She was bent double, her forehead nearly resting on the bar of the seat in front, her arms wrapped tightly around her middle. She wore gloves without fingers and the scarlet paint on her bitten nails was chipped and worn. I was about to ask her if I could put the bag on the floor when she looked up, her face a mass of wrinkles, her mouth sunken over gums she bared in a vicious grin. I stepped back, nearly colliding with two schoolgirls who were chatting in the aisle.

"Watch out," one said, pulling her leather knapsack away from my feet.

I looked down at the old woman. She was bent over again, swaying back and forth, singing without words a high-pitched complaint. At least Great-Aunt Beatrice had had her house and her cats, as well as neighbours who watched her with attention, if not with love, who may have called her a witch but noted her comings and goings. I wondered what fortune she would have told for me.

FOUR

Bonnie Hazlitt came out of her apartment when she heard the sound of my key in the door across the hall.

"How's the mystery aunt? I've been waiting and waiting for you to get home. Come in and tell me all about her."

"She's dead."

"Dead?" She sagged back against her door.

"It's not that big a deal," I said hastily. "It happened before I got there. She'd fallen down the stairs in her house and died. A neighbour called the police. Her lawyer turned up while I was talking to some detectives and he knew about me. He wanted to talk. That's what took so long."

"So you never got to meet her? That's awful." Bonnie rushed across the hall to hug me. Although I'm by no means tall, her head barely reached my shoulders. I don't like being hugged, especially by casual friends. There's something about touch, the too easy assumption that it means intimacy and love. I stood stiff, hands at my side.

Bonnie dropped her arms. She sniffled and swept her fist across her eyes. "Look at me, crying again. I hate it, the way I'm always bursting into tears. My heart's too soft, that's what Robin always says."

Or too bruised, I thought, not for the first time and not out loud. "I have to phone Will. I promised I'd call as soon as I got back."

She looked at her watch. "He'll still be working. Why don't you come in and have a cup of tea? You look like you need it."

"I don't feel that bad," I insisted. "It's not as though she meant anything to me. She never wanted anything to do with me until it was too late. If you want to know the truth, I feel like I've won a lottery, sort of."

"You're the long lost heir, right? You've come into a fortune." She clapped her hands.

"Not exactly."

"You can't leave me in suspense like this." She grabbed my hand and pulled me into her apartment. "You've got to tell me the whole story."

I gave up. There was no stopping Bonnie once she determined on some course of action. She was a friend of a friend, a graduate student like me, but of Art History, not Literature. She had come to one of our pub gatherings last year, one of those nights when we let off steam about our thesis supervisors, the slim chances of employment when (if) we finished our degrees, and the difficulties of our varied living situations. I was then trying to find an affordable apartment downtown to escape the horrors of suburbia. She knew a neighbour who was getting married and needed to find someone to sublet his place; she invited me to visit the next day, introduced us, and arranged the deal.

The fact that she lived right across the hall seemed a piece of luck at first. Absorbed as I was with classes, research, and papers, I was sometimes lonely. My friend warned me that Bonnie could be a bit demanding, but I figured that, since she was working part-time at the Royal Ontario Museum as well as studying, and had a live-in boyfriend, she would be pretty busy herself. However, her boyfriend worked long shifts and she would, too often, come across the hall, looking for company. Sometimes, when she came knocking at the door, I would sit frozen in my chair, pen poised over paper, breath held as if she could hear my heart pumping. She'd go away, but ten minutes later would be back, the soft repeated rapping insistently upsetting. If I answered her second or third attack, she would assume I'd been in the bathroom or on the phone. She was not good at taking hints that I liked my own company. For her, solitude was isolation.

Her apartment was the twin of mine. I went straight to the dining table which was positioned in front of the picture window that looked down on Spadina. Only three floors above the street, the traffic noise was a constant hum and occasional heart-stopping squeal. I pulled out one of the high-backed chairs and sat.

"What are you making for dinner?" I asked. "It smells delicious."

Bonnie plunked down a tray laden with tea pot, cups, and a plate of chocolate brownies. The pot and cups were glazed in gradations of blue, from almost black at the base to a nearly white rim. Each handle was a braided twist that incorporated all the shades in an intricate interplay of strands.

"Ratatouille," she said, "one of Robin's meatless favourites. I thought I'd surprise him with it." She sighed. "There's lots of it. You want to stay to eat? No sense in it going to waste."

"He has to work late?" I asked her.

"Yeah." She poured the tea.

"Again?"

"You know how it is."

I knew. "It goes with the territory. We're lucky, being in school. We may have to stay up all night writing papers, but at least we can sleep in in the morning. Clock-punchers don't get much choice."

"It's nothing to joke about. He works far too hard. They take advantage of him."

"Who?"

"The kids, the other social workers, the administrators. He cares too much. He even brings them here, you know, kids just off the street: hookers and drug users, it doesn't matter to him. He'll say the hostel's full and they need a place to stay. Some of them have lice." She shivered.

"Isn't that what you fell in love with? His goodness?"

"Taking in strays, you mean? Like me?"

"You weren't exactly needy."

"But straying," she tried to laugh. "Harold would say I'm getting my comeuppance. My mother says, if you make a bed, you have to lie in it."

"How is your mother?"

"You're changing the subject."

I sighed. "You knew what he was like when you decided to move here with him. And you know he only works so many extra shifts because you need the money."

"I didn't leave Harold and the kids to sit in this dump weekend after weekend by myself."

"You've got your thesis."

She poked the stack of papers piled on the end of the table so viciously that they teetered. I caught them before they fell.

"Sorry." Bonnie bit her lip. "I don't know what good it's going to do me. There are no jobs anyway, with the recession."

"Tell me about it." I readied myself to stand. "There were only three tenure-track jobs advertised in all of Canada in my field this past year and they were all in the prairies. Sometimes, I wonder why we bother."

"Don't go yet." Bonnie grabbed my hand across the table. "I won't talk about myself any more, I promise. You haven't had a brownie yet. Try one." She picked up one herself and licked at the icing. "I'm supposed to be on a diet, you know."

"Why do you keep doing this to yourself? It's a roller coaster: you lose a few pounds, go back to eating normally, and the weight just comes back."

"I know, I know. You and Robin are the same. *You look fine the way you are.* You wouldn't say that if you were me." She grabbed a handful of flesh from her midriff and shook it in disgust. "I hate the way I look. You should have seen me when I was sixteen."

"Isn't that the year you were anorexic?"

"I just didn't like to eat. My mother's a lousy cook." She ran her fingers through her blonde hair, lifting it high and then letting it cascade down her back. "And I'm thinking of cutting my hair all off too. Get one of those mushroom cuts, you know?"

"So you and Robin will look like the Bobbsey Twins? Come on, Bonn, that long straight hair suits you."

"I just want a change." She rolled her hair into a tight knot and held it on top of her head. When I smiled, she let it go. "Anyway," she continued, "tell me everything. Your aunt first. No, the fortune."

I circled the rim of my mug with one finger. "This is beautiful," I stalled. "Who made it?"

"Me."

"I didn't know you were a potter."

She shrugged. "Ryan was into making mud pies, so I thought I would too."

"You shouldn't put yourself down like that." I picked up the pot and turned it to admire the wildflowers delicately etched into the glaze. "These are really special. I love this shade of blue."

"Everything I made is blue: dishes, bowls, mugs, what-have-you. Harold likes to have things match and his house has blue carpets. Besides, my mood then was always blue, sometimes a little lighter, mostly like this." And she traced the navy lines that underlay all the pieces, the dark shadow behind every daisy.

I sipped the tea. It was fragrant with cinnamon and had a strong cidery aftertaste. Bonnie put her cup down and shook her hair free of her face.

"Enough about me. Now, tell."

"There's not much. And the fortune's not money, but land."

"In the city? Her house? Lucky you."

"No, no, not the house. It's in pretty bad shape, anyway, probably cost more than it's worth to fix up. She had fifty cats living with her, can you imagine?"

"Fifty? How big was the house?"

"Not big enough. There were litter pans everywhere. It'll be impossible to get the smell out."

"So where's this land?"

"In Haliburton. Have you ever heard of Cook's Lake?"

"You're joking! Are you sure you've got the name right? Cook's Lake?"

"Apparently it's named for the family."

"It seems amazing, but I've been there, you know. Harold's sister's husband has a friend who has land up there and we went to visit a couple of times before the kids were born. And one of Robin's runaways..." she paused.

"Yeah?" I encouraged.

She shook her head. "I shouldn't have said that. It's confidential. Robin's always warning me I talk too much. But it's one of the places he's been visiting lately. On business," she added, hastily. "You're really lucky, Rosie. It's beautiful country up there."

"With my luck, I've inherited all the swampy bits," I laughed.

"You never know. It could be worth a fortune. Cottage land is at such a premium these days. My brother-in-law was always talking about how his friend's property could be developed; it had enough shoreline for a whole subdivision of cottages."

"Which are probably there by now. What I've got is one hundred acres of family land. My grandfather left it to my aunt with the understanding that she was to pass it on to me. And if I don't want it, I'm supposed to give it to the government. For the birds." I giggled, stifling a yawn. "What a day."

"Boy, if I came into land like that, I'd sell it and take the money, and leave."

"Where would you go?"

"Paris, the south of France, Tahiti. I'd go to a real art school. I've always wanted to be an artist."

"What about Robin? The kids?"

She shrugged. "It might be nice to be really free..." Her voice trailed into silence. She shook herself. "What do you mean: if you don't want it? If you don't want to live there, you could sell it."

"It's all very complicated. I don't know if I should take it."

"Do you have any idea what land up there is worth these days? Especially if it has waterfront. Does it?"

"Markham said something about a thousand feet of shoreline."

"Wow! You're in the money!" She reached over and shook my hand, then blinked, puzzled. "Did you say Markham? Not Roger Markham?"

"Don't tell me he's your brother-in-law. Ex-brother-in-law, I mean."

"Small world." Bonnie's lips twitched in an awkward grin.

"You're kidding."

She shook her head. "I can't seem to get away from Harold, no matter how much I try. How is old Roger these days? I haven't seen him or talked to him since Harold and I split up."

"He wasn't very friendly."

"That's Roger, all right. He and Harold were a perfect pair: supercilious and condescending. Not that I'm prejudiced, of course." She laughed. "I could never understand how Ellen could stand him. But then she's Harold's sister. Anyone who grew up with Harold would be used to chauvinism. Or immune to it."

"I won't have to deal with him again, I hope. It's his uncle who's my aunt's lawyer. Markham was just along for the ride."

"Roger has never, in living memory, done anything without a reason. And that reason usually has something to do with making money. You'd better watch out for him. Maybe he's representing someone else in the family. Did your aunt have children?"

"That's funny." I thought suddenly of the picture of the girl holding a cat, and how quickly the lawyers left once Gianelli started questioning them about other heirs. "No one said anything about her own family, just talked about my grandfather and my parents."

"I wonder if she married a Baker on purpose, just to change her name that way — from Cook to Baker. Would you call that a step up in the social scale?" She bit into another brownie.

"We hardly talked about her at all, even though we were sitting in her house and she'd died right there in the front hallway." I shivered. "I wish I had had a chance to talk to her."

"So why did she leave you this cottage? And why don't you want it? I'd give my eyeteeth to have a place to go to, to get out of this city in the summer. Or to sell, and have all that lovely money to spend."

"She didn't leave me the cottage, my grandfather did. He didn't get along with my mother..."

"Sounds like my family." She picked up another brownie, caught my eye, and placed it on the plate again. "Do you think there's any such thing as a happy family?"

"Not that I know of. Anyway, that's why I don't think I should keep the property. Mom hated the Cooks so much, she even told me they were all dead so that I'd stop asking questions about them. If I took something from them, it would be like denying her, saying that all her sacrifice was for nothing."

"Now, wait just a minute." Bonnie stood up and began to pace, her hair swinging back and forth. "First, your mother isn't here to be hurt by whatever you do or don't do. Second, perhaps leaving you the property was a way for your grandfather to make up to you, something he couldn't do while he was still alive. Third, land is land. Someone has to own it. Why not you?"

"I don't feel right about it."

Bonnie groaned.

We watched while the sky outside deepened to the silvery gray that passed for darkness in the heart of the city. I pushed my mug away and stood. "I'm beat. I want to get out of these clothes and have a long, hot bath."

"How's the studying going?"

"Don't ask."

"Has a date been set for your exams yet?"

"End of June." I shivered. "I've been dreaming about high school again: Grade 13 and I have to write a physics exam but I've skipped classes all year. If I fail, I won't be able to go to university. And of course, I get the time wrong and can't find the room. I'm walking down a long empty hall in squeaky shoes; all the doors are closed and I know I'm late."

"I hate those dreams," Bonnie sympathized.

"Stupid thing is, I didn't even take physics in my last year in high school."

"Drink hot milk before you go to bed. It always works for Ryan." She bit her lip on the name.

Another minefield. I sneaked a glance at my watch: past seven. Will would be wondering what had happened to me.

Bonnie buried her face in a tea towel. When she looked up, her eyes were suspiciously bright, but there were no signs of tears. "I'm sick of crying over this. Robin says I have to let go, that there's no way we can get custody."

"I thought you'd worked that out," I ventured. "Didn't you settle on reasonable visiting rights?"

"Reasonable! One weekend once a month in Ottawa. It's totally unfair. They're my kids. Ryan's nine, old enough to recognize the lies, but Megan's only four. How's she supposed to ever get to know me? She was just a baby when I left, when I had to leave. I'm just a visitor to her."

"Aren't you exaggerating just a little? She seemed pretty happy with you and Robin when I met her here last fall."

"My mother was here too," Bonnie said. "My own children don't know me." She sniffled.

"I don't know what to say that I haven't said before." I stood up. I wanted to go, but couldn't leave her here like this. "I never even knew I had a father until I was her age, and then my mother wouldn't talk about him. I imagined all kinds of things. At least you're there in her life. She'll get to know you..."

"She hides under the blankets when I come to get her. She cries all the way to my mother's house and when we get there, she won't let me touch her. Every weekend it's the same: by the time she's willing to be friends with me again, it's time for her to go home. Sometimes I wonder if it's worth the effort."

"Bonnie!"

"It's so hard," she cried. "Ryan can be so rude, you wouldn't believe it. It's all Harold's fault, the stories he tells them about me."

"You don't know that he does that," I pointed out. "He is a teacher, after all. He must deal with kids from broken homes all the time. Surely he wouldn't try to make the situation more difficult for them by criticizing you. And he does let you visit."

"On his terms."

"Maybe it's what the kids need right now, the security of being in their own place..."

"It's been three years," Bonnie retorted. "It would be so much better if I could have them with me all the time."

"What about Robin? How does he feel about them? And what about your job? And your degree? And where would they go to school?"

"You're as bad as my mother," she sighed. "She says it serves me right, I should never have left them. What does she know? Her marriage was a disaster from day one and she only made it worse for all of us by staying in it."

"Do you have to take them to your mother's house?"

"I can't afford a hotel. And none of my so-called friends will speak to me. They all blame me for leaving Harold, the 'perfect husband and provider.' If they only knew. Do you know what he used to do?"

"I don't want to hear this, Bonnie."

She paid no attention. "He'd put white threads on the kitchen floor in the corners or under the shelves. If they were still there after I housecleaned, he'd make me scrub the floor again, on my hands and knees, with a toothbrush. He was real tricky about it: he didn't do it every week, so I was never sure if they'd be there or not. Sometimes, he pretended to find them in places I knew I'd double-checked. He said it was for my own good. He said it was to make sure I kept his house clean enough for his children to grow up in."

"How could you live with such a man?"

"I couldn't. That's why meeting Robin was so wonderful. He really cared about me, my wants, my needs. I didn't believe a man could be so understanding."

"Don't any of your friends like him?"

"They're mostly Harold's friends, from work. All they see is how young Robin is. Ten years difference isn't that big a deal, is it? If it was reversed and he was the one who was older, no one would think anything of it."

"You shouldn't let what other people think bother you so much. If you and Robin are happy together..."

"And what about my kids?" she interrupted. "It's his fault they can't come here any more. Harold used to let my mother bring them down here to visit, if I couldn't get up to Ottawa. Then last Thanksgiving — you heard the fuss she made when Robin brought that street kid home for dinner. The whole city heard her."

"It wasn't that bad..."

"You should have seen her face when Megan picked a cockroach out of that boy's backpack! I thought she'd die on the spot." She affected a kind of giggle that turned into a gulping sob. She jumped up from the table and ran into the bathroom.

I carried the tea things back into the kitchen and then stood in the little hall, unsure what to do next. The front door opened.

"Hey, Rosie, how's it going?" Robin dropped a canvas bag on the floor. A half-peeled orange fell out along with an assortment of pencils and a dog-eared paperback.

"You got home after all." I shook his hand. Robin Elgin was a bean-pole of a man, over six feet tall and thin to boot. In his late twenties, he was already going bald and perhaps for that reason, or perhaps to camouflage his full lips and weak chin, he sported a full moustache and beard. Today, as on every working day, he wore a tweed sports jacket over a turtleneck shirt and blue jeans.

The toilet flushed. He pushed his glasses back up his nose

and nodded towards the back of the apartment. "She all right?" he whispered.

"A bit upset. She started talking about the kids again."

He grimaced. "It's a bad scene."

Bonnie joined us. "You're home," she said. She reached up to peck him on the cheek. "I thought you had to go up north on business?"

"I was going to leave straight from work, they kept me so late. But I wanted to see you first. We should talk." He glanced at me. "I guess it can wait." He slipped by me into the kitchen. "Great, dinner's ready. I'm starving."

"I won't stay. I really must go and phone Will." I opened the door. "You'll be all right?"

"Sure." She scuffed her toe. "Sorry about all that. I thought I was over it."

"It takes time." What a dumb thing to say, I thought savagely. But what else could I say?

"Yeah. It's just ... things are piling up, tuition, exams, those visits to Ottawa. I'm pretty stressed out right now. But listen, are you going to go to your aunt's funeral? Do you want me to come with you? Or do you think Will might come down for it?"

"I haven't thought about it yet. I guess Mr. Ross will let me know when it is. I'll talk to you when I hear from him." I paused, one hand on the outer door knob. Robin had come back to the hall, a pot in one hand and fork in the other.

"This is terrific," he said, holding the pot towards me. "Want to try some?"

"I really have to go." I edged out into the hall.

"Do you have to eat out of the pot like that?" Bonnie complained, her voice rising. "Are you in such a hurry you can't even sit and eat like a civilized human being? You're worse than Ryan."

I could see Robin flush. "You know I don't have much time, especially if you want me back before morning."

"All right." She pushed him towards the kitchen. "At least go into the other room so Rosie doesn't have to watch the way you eat. I'll be with you in a moment." She turned back to me. "That's all right, then? You will call if you need me?" She began closing the door.

"Yeah. Thanks for the tea."

She nodded. I listened to the click of the safety lock and then the fading whine of her voice. What a pair they were.

The phone was ringing as I unlocked my own door, but had stopped before I reached it. It must have been Will. I longed to talk to him, someone who wasn't so obsessed with his own problems that he wouldn't listen to mine. I wouldn't have to explain my desolation to him, how my grief at losing my aunt before even meeting her warred with my excitement about discovering that I did have roots — and not only roots, but family land.

While counting the telephone rings at home, I allowed myself to fantasize, picturing both an imposing rural mansion with two bathrooms and a sauna, perched on rocks above a white sand beach, and a one-room log cabin nestled in pine trees by a rocky shore. I put down the phone. Will must be out walking Sadie. Sadie will love it up north, I thought.

I lit a candle and placed it on the toilet seat, turned the hot water on full and poured a generous amount of orange cream oil into the tub. Fragrant steam filled the small bathroom. I left the water running while I went to dial Will again. A fragment of tune repeated itself in my head, a song my mother used to sing when we walked back together, hand in hand, from an outing. "Show me the way to go home," I sang aloud.

This time, Will answered my call.

FIVE

I couldn't find any notice of Aunt Beatrice's funeral, nor was there any mention, even in the most sensational local paper, of the peculiar circumstances of her strange death and her house full of cats. I waited a couple of days before calling the offices of Ross, Armour and Markham. The receptionist had a thin, nasal voice which sang through the company name with an irritating lilt. When I asked for Mr. Ross, she said he wasn't in. I hesitated before mentioning Roger Markham. There was a long wait before he answered his phone. I listened to a whining violin rendition of "Hey Jude." Just as a chorus of horns broke out in fanfare, Markham came on the line.

"What can I do for you, Ms. Cairns?" His voice was brusque but polite, the voice of a busy man interrupted in the middle of important work.

"I'm phoning to ask about Aunt Beatrice," I said. "I'd like to go to her funeral."

"She didn't have one. At her own request it was a very private affair. She was cremated this morning."

"Oh." I felt bereft. I'd never met her, and now had been denied the chance to mourn. Although, of course, it wouldn't have been the woman I missed, but the chance to be rooted in family. Ah well, that was nothing new.

"I imagine," Markham drawled, "that you want to know about the land."

"As a matter of fact, yes."

"No big surprise."

"Pardon?"

"I wondered how long it would take you to call."

"What do you mean by that?"

"Nothing," he snickered.

"I didn't go looking for her, you know," I retorted. "It was Aunt Beatrice who wrote to me. If she hadn't, I never would have heard about her or the family land."

"But now that you've heard about it, you can't wait to get your hands on it."

"Mr. Markham, you're really out of line."

There was a pause. When he spoke again, his voice had softened considerably. "I'm sorry," he apologized. "It's been one of those days. What does your husband think about all this? I imagine he sees the advantage in selling while the market's still hot."

"My husband really has nothing to do with it. It's my land."

"He's putting you through school, isn't he? From what I understand, his business is pretty small. Carpenter, isn't he?"

"He's a renovation contractor, and I'm paying my own way. Although that's our business, not yours."

"I'd be happy to make it my business. I have a client..."

"I'm sure you do. I'm not ready to discuss the property till I've seen it. My grandfather and my aunt wanted me to have it. I should at least visit it before I decide whether to keep it or not."

"You shouldn't leave it too late. Spring's the best time for cottage sales."

"What about the bird sanctuary?"

"That's not legally binding. Once the deed is in your hands, it's yours to do with as you want. I have a lot of experience in the area of estate planning and so on. This could prove quite a windfall towards a comfortable retirement. I'm more than willing to advise you..."

"I'll keep that in mind."

"You do that, Ms. Cairns. You do that." He hung up.

I replaced the receiver and sat for a time with my hand on it. We had always expected to inherit the Cairns family cottage. Will had so many good memories of his childhood up there, and we had managed to spend a couple of weeks there each summer. What would we need with two such places? And the money would be nice — like winning a lottery, the sale of one hundred acres of cottage land would finance the kind of vacations we only dreamed of now. As for my grandfather's wishes, I owed him nothing — nothing at all.

On Thursday, the buzz of the intercom interrupted me in the middle of washing the bathroom floor. I was supposed to be studying; my texts and notes were neatly arranged on the round table I used both for dining and working. There were three pens, a sharpened pencil, an eraser, and a new yellow highlighter waiting beside the stack of books. I'd sat for an hour staring at the pages before giving up. I hated studying. The floor did need a wash. I must admit, though, I didn't in the least mind the interruption. I stood the mop in the pail and went to answer the summons.

"This is Hunter, Ma'am," the voice crackled into the room. "Mr. Ross's driver. Mr. Ross would like you to step down to see him for a few moments."

I pushed my hair back from my face. My hands were red and swollen from the hot water. I knew I should wear gloves, but the ones I had had holes in them.

"Perhaps he'd like to come up for tea." As soon as I said it, I regretted the invitation. Although I kept my apartment clean, it was not very tidy: newspapers and books occupied much of the couch and the floor around it. Since the bookcase I'd brought from home was too small, more books were piled along the wall behind the rocking chair which was draped with a couple of afghans knitted by Will's mother in peculiar shades of green and pink. One coffee mug was on the floor by this chair; another sat on top of the TV along with a dying English ivy plant and a stack of TV guides. Because I didn't buy snack foods — the only way to avoid eating too many cookies or chips was not to have them available — I had nothing to offer by way of refreshment. My mother would have been appalled. I could make tea or fresh coffee. I always bought good coffee from the Second Cup. Hazelnut Cream was my favourite.

"Mr. Ross would prefer that you come down," the driver said. "He's a little indisposed."

"I'll be there in a minute, then."

I glanced out the window. The rain that had been threatening all morning was falling now in gray sheets. Streetlights gleamed and cars sprayed the sidewalks as they hissed by. Parked by the hydrant in front of my building was the limousine, its hazard lights lazily flashing.

As usual my umbrella was not in the closet where it should have been. I debated hunting for it. Had I brought it back from the university last week? My old yellow slicker was stuck in a corner behind a parka and long wool coat. I put it on over the blue sweatshirt and pants I wore around the house. I almost forgot to exchange slippers for running shoes.

The intercom buzzed again. "I'm coming," I shouted into it.

Downstairs in the lobby, two men pointedly ignored each other: the driver, Hunter, and Roger Markham. Even in the tiny front entrance area, they had found a good three feet of space to separate them. Avoiding each other, they both watched the elevator through the glass partition that separated the entrance from the lobby. I always used the stairs: the elevator was not very reliable and I had a horror of being stuck for an hour or two with one of the weird, wired kids who lived on the upper floors. It was bad enough refusing their constant offers of dope deals; the thought of having to actually make conversation with one of them was unendurable. Besides, the exercise did me good.

Hunter stepped forward as I pushed open the glass door.

"Mr. Ross is waiting," he said.

"Just a minute," Markham interrupted. "I'd like a word with you first."

"Aren't you with your uncle?" I asked.

Before he could answer, Hunter spoke, "Mr. Markham arrived a minute ago. Mr. Ross will be getting impatient." He opened the outer door and unfurled an enormous black umbrella.

"I'll come with you," Markham moved to follow me out the door.

Hunter barred his way. "Mr. Ross's business is with Mrs. Cairns alone. He won't be happy to see you here. He might start asking questions."

Whatever threat was implied in that statement was suffi-
cient to make Markham back down.

"I'll wait here then," he muttered. He leaned against the
wall of mail boxes, his eyes on his feet. I was going to let him
into the lobby where he could perch on one of the orange nau-
gahyde chairs the superintendent kept forgetting to dust, but
had no time to unlock the door for him.

"This way, Ma'am." Hunter's pressure on my elbow steered
me out and across the sidewalk. The door opened and I was
pushed politely but firmly into the back seat. Hunter remained
outside, his back to the car, the umbrella casting a deep shade
over him.

So this was what the inside of a limousine looked like. The
long seat was upholstered in gray leather; gray carpeting covered the floors, walls, and ceiling. Under the tinted window
that divided the front of the car from the back was a long console flanked by two smaller leather seats, both facing backwards. The console held a telephone, a small television, and a
silver tray with a cut glass decanter which looked nearly full of
amber liquid, probably scotch whiskey, and two glasses. A
round silver bowl held a pot pourri of dried roses whose scent
vied with the pervasive odor of Vicks Vaporub. All the comforts
of home, I thought. When I sat, my rubber raincoat squeaked
against the leather.

Mr. Ross coughed. In spite of the warm spring rain, he was
still bundled in his fur-collared coat and hat. A long plaid scarf
had been wrapped around his neck so that only his eyes and
the tip of his nose peeked forth. The way he sat hunched over
his cane reminded me irresistibly of Alistair Sims as Scrooge. I
wondered what role I had to play: Tiny Tim, or the beggar girl
in the snow.

"Mrs. Cairns," he nodded at me, "good of you to come
down to see me. I find it difficult getting in and out of the car.
Rheumatism." He thumped his stick on the floor.

"I was sorry that Mrs. Baker didn't have a funeral. I would
have liked to say good-bye to her."

"She had requested that there be no funeral. Under the circumstances, it was best that everything was kept quiet."

"I would have liked to go."

He shifted uneasily in his place. "I brought this over for

you. It's what you're waiting for, I imagine."

He lifted one hand from his stick and reached over to the console, aiming for a yellow legal size envelope next to the tray. It was too far; I was afraid he'd topple over.

"I'll get it," I murmured.

He sank back.

The envelope was thick with papers. My name was written on it in the shaky, cursive script that I'd last seen on my aunt's invitation.

"It's from Beatrice," the old man said. "The deed is in there, and a map, and the key. It's all yours."

"I don't have to sign anything?"

He shook his head. "The proper enquiries have been made. You are who you say you are. Who I know you are."

I felt the hard ridges of the key under my fingers. Family property: I wondered if there would be pictures there. That reminded me. "Mr. Ross, did my aunt have children of her own? Do I have any cousins?"

"No concern of yours," he snapped. "The place is yours and everything in it."

"I'd really like to know," I pleaded. "All those pictures in her house: what's happened to them? And all her things?"

He blew out his breath. "Questions, questions. Worse than an old woman you are."

"You're not being fair to me," I insisted. "Aunt Beatrice was going to tell me everything. Do I have cousins?"

"One," he sighed. "Beatrice's granddaughter, Marilyn Finch."

"Does she live here in the city?"

He shook his head. "Never has. Her mother married an American. She lives in the Southern States somewhere. One of the Carolinas. Roger would know. He takes care of the trust fund Beatrice's husband set up for his family."

"Does she know about me?"

"Of course she knows about you. Now. Beatrice said she wrote to her at Christmas and told her the whole story. She inherits the house — she won't get much for it, I'm afraid. You saw what condition it's in. Roger is taking care of all that for her."

"What does she do?"

He shifted uneasily on the seat. "What does it matter?" he waved a hand dismissively. "She never bothered with her grandmother except when she wanted the cottage for vacations. Never visited Beatrice in the city and made sure her time up north didn't overlap with her grandmother's weeks there. She didn't even bother coming up when we informed her about Beatrice's death. I doubt she wants to meet you. Especially now that you've got the cottage." He chuckled. "Serves her right. Probably planned to sell the land and pocket the money. No flies on Beatrice, you've got to say that for her." He cocked his head. "I wonder, now, if it wasn't so much guilt about not carrying out her brother's wish to give the land to you, but revenge on Marilyn that led her to contact you. Could be, could be." He cackled.

I shifted on the seat. The raincoat squeaked against the leather. "You can't just leave it like that. You have to tell me something about her. Is she married? Does she have kids?"

"Ask Roger," the old man muttered. "He's the one who deals with her."

"I will," I said. "He's waiting for me now." I nodded towards the building.

"Roger is?" Mr. Ross looked up in surprise. The cane slipped from his hands and fell to the floor. I picked it up. He took it from me quite roughly and used the rubber end to bang on the window. I leaned back into the seat, away from its erratic waving.

Hunter opened the door and looked in. "Yes, sir?"

"What's Mr. Markham doing here?" the old man demanded.

"I'm afraid I don't know, sir. He arrived just after we did. You didn't see him going in?"

"Of course not. Go and ask him what he's doing here. This is none of his business. I thought I had made that quite plain."

Hunter closed the door with a quiet thud. Mr. Ross wheezed heavily. I could hear him muttering to himself but couldn't make out the words. A couple of minutes passed in silence. The door opened again.

"He says it's something to do with Dr. Finch, some personal things about the family she thought Mrs. Cairns would like to know."

Mr. Ross glared at his driver for a moment, then nodded. His whole body seemed to shrink into his coat. I caught Hunter's worried look. It was time for me to go.

"Thank you for bringing me these papers yourself," I said. "I guess I should be going."

The old man waved one twisted hand in farewell. Hunter reached for my elbow to help me out of the car. I turned my face up to the sweet rain, glad to be out of that cloying atmosphere. Mr. Ross banged on the window. The driver reopened the door.

"Mrs. Cairns," the old man called. "One moment please."

I leaned back inside the car, steadying myself with one hand on the roof.

"Remember," Mr. Ross said. "your grandfather's wishes. If you don't want to use the cottage yourself, the land is to go the province. It's not to be sold, you hear."

"I wasn't planning on selling it."

"It's not to be sold," Mr. Ross repeated. His cough shook his whole body. Tears streamed down his cheeks.

Hunter eased the door shut. "I'll see you in, ma'am," he said.

"Will he be all right?" I nodded toward the car.

"Happens," Hunter replied. "He's got an inhaler in there. And a spittoon. Doesn't like people to see him use it. He's got pride for an old fellow."

We reached the door. Markham was reading a newspaper he'd pulled from a stack on the floor. He began refolding it when he saw us. I was about to go inside, when Hunter stopped me with a slight pressure on the elbow.

"Watch out for him," he whispered.

"Who? Mr. Markham? Why?"

Before he could answer, Markham opened the door. "That took long enough," he grumbled. He eyed the envelope I clutched in my hands. "Hunter, you can leave now."

"Yes sir," the driver snapped a salute.

Markham flushed.

I stifled a grin. "Thanks for the umbrella, Mr. Hunter. And the advice." I held out my hand to him. After a moment, he shook it, then turned and left.

"What advice was that?" Markham asked.

I just shook my head.

"Shall we go upstairs then?" He nodded at the door.

"Tell me your business first."

"It's to your advantage." He saw that I wasn't about to invite him in. He sighed. "You know your aunt had a granddaughter? Dr. Marilyn Finch."

"Yes. I didn't know she was a doctor, though."

"Not a medical doctor. A professor. Like you want to be."

"What's her field?"

"What difference does that make?"

"I'm curious."

"Archaeology."

"What university?"

"She's not at a university any more. She's freelance, does consultations for developers, some museums, collectors. That kind of thing. Anyway, she wants to make an offer for the land."

"Why doesn't she make it in person, then?" I snapped.

"She lives in the States, in North Carolina as a matter of fact, when she's not on the road. Her work involves a lot of field locations. She asked me to talk to you about the cottage, to explain her sentimental attachment. She's always thought of the place as her one true home. You can imagine how she felt when she found out her grandmother had left it to you, a stranger."

"She's known about it for nearly five months. Aunt Beatrice told her at Christmas, your uncle said. Why hasn't she bothered to get in touch with me if she's so concerned?"

"Mrs. Baker simply told her of your existence. We didn't know about the bequest until after she died."

"I thought you looked after the estate?"

"I only administer the trust that Beatrice's husband and father provided. My uncle kept the wills in his personal safe. She was more than a client to him, as he keeps reminding me."

"And what is Dr. Finch's relationship to you?"

He flushed. "I will ignore that remark. You may want to know that she has asked me to fax her a copy of both your grandfather's and her grandmother's wills. She doesn't want to cause trouble, but she's talking about contesting them."

"Is that a threat?"

He held up both hands. "No, no. I'm sure we can come to

some amicable arrangement."

"I haven't even had a chance to look at these papers." I waved the envelope at him. "I won't say yes or no. I plan to go up to Cook's Lake soon and see the place. After that we can talk."

"She's willing to buy the land," he said. "Five hundred thousand dollars. Cash."

"Half a million dollars? That's an awful lot of money!"

He shrugged. "It's worth it to her. Are you interested?"

"I'll have to think about it." I weighed the envelope in my hand. "I don't think I can. There's that stipulation my grandfather put in, that if I don't want the land, I have to give it to the province."

"That's not legally binding," Markham said patiently. He shifted from one foot to the other. Obviously he would have preferred to be sitting comfortably in my apartment. I just wanted to get rid of him so that I could get a good look at what Mr. Ross had given me.

"Your uncle insists on it," I said.

"It's only to your cousin," his voice rose. "It's not like it's going out of the family. She has more claim on the place than you do, sentimental and otherwise."

"What do you mean?"

"There's a question about your parents' marriage. How legal it was."

"They got married in England. In a church. My mother showed me pictures."

"Pictures can be faked. That church was destroyed in the blitz — if it existed at all."

"Just what are you implying?" I stood very still to try to stop the trembling that rose in waves from my knees to my lips. I blinked back sudden tears.

"It's a question of legitimacy," Markham went on. "Whether you really are your grandfather's heir or not."

"My father was George Cook," I retorted. "That's been proven."

"His name is on your birth certificate, true."

"Your uncle is perfectly satisfied with my right to the family property."

"My uncle is old."

"I've had enough." I reached past him for the door handle.

He grabbed my arm. "Let's quit pretending," he said. "You can't tell me you're not interested in the money. Everyone's interested in money. Think of what you could do with half a million dollars. I'm sure your husband would."

"Leave Will out of this."

"Why would you want to be saddled with a few acres of rock in the middle of nowhere? The taxes are high and there's the upkeep of the house. It's not a free ride; a lot of costs go along with owning land."

"Please let go of my arm." I refused to look at him.

"You okay, Rosie?" Bonnie pushed in from outside, a sack of groceries in each hand. She shook her head to dislodge the hood of her raincoat. "What are you doing here?" she demanded.

Markham dropped my arm to brush at some drops of water that spotted the sleeve of his overcoat. "Talking to Ms. Cairns."

"About me?" she glared at him. "Did Harold send you to spy on me?"

"Harold doesn't send me anywhere," Markham said. "I'm not interested in the sordid little details of your life. I have business with Ms. Cairns."

"Watch out for him then," Bonnie said to me. "Snake is his middle name. He's probably trying to chisel you out of that land your aunt left you."

"Now, just a minute," Markham protested.

She ignored him. "Open the door for me, will you?" she asked me.

I unlocked it. She elbowed her way through, then turned back to stare at us through the glass. The elevator door slid open. She ignored it.

"Bonnie's waiting," I said to Markham. "I think our business is concluded, don't you?"

He controlled his temper with a visible effort. "I forgot she lived in this building."

"She lives right across the hall from me."

He shook his head. "How lucky for you. I'd keep away from her if I were you. She's a bit..." He patted his temple with one finger.

"Funny thing, she says the same about you," I retorted.

"What's she been saying?" he demanded, his brows furrowing. "She doesn't know anything about me."

"You're her brother-in-law."

"I was. Past tense. Anyway, she's got nothing to do with why I'm here. I want to discuss the property. I can understand your curiosity to see the place. I can appreciate that." He took a deep breath. "But you must understand your cousin's position. She loves the cottage, she needs it to escape to. It's part of her identity. You wouldn't want to take that away from her, would you?"

"If it's so important to her, why doesn't she ask me herself?" It seemed such a reasonable question, I didn't mind repeating it.

"She is sensitive to the awkwardness of the situation. She thought I'd be better as a go-between. Until things are settled. She even suggested that she'd be willing to rent it from you, until you're ready to sell."

"You're selling your cottage?" Bonnie broke in, her nose almost pressed to the glass door. "When did you decide that?"

"I haven't decided anything," I shouted. "Look, I'll go through these papers tonight. This is the long weekend: Will and I were going up north tomorrow anyway; we'll stop at the lake and look at it. We'll get in touch with you after that."

"Dr. Finch won't leave the offer open for long," Markham said. "You might not get such a good deal from someone else."

"Don't push me," I said. "I'll make up my own mind in my own time. If my cousin is so anxious to deal with me, she should contact me in person. If she can't be bothered even to speak to me, why should I care if her grandmother's death has spoiled her vacation?"

"She's a very busy woman," Markham muttered.

"Well, so am I." I slammed the inner door shut and stalked to the elevators. Both doors opened for a change. Bonnie got in one, I took the other. I rode it to the top of the building, then back down to the third floor. The hall was empty. Good. I didn't want to talk to Bonnie right then, to listen to more complaints about Harold and his treatment of her. I had my own problems to deal with. I was able to get inside my apartment without interruption. There was a map in the envelope, along with a thick file of legal papers. And photographs. I lunged for the phone to dial Will.

SIX

Every twenty-fourth of May holiday weekend for the past fifteen years, Will and I have gone up to his parents' cottage on Lake of Bays. While Will works taking down the shutters, repairing ice damage to the dock, putting in the water lines and raking deadfall to the compost heap, I'm indoors, washing every plate and pot and spoon, checking for mice nests in cupboard drawers, and beating the rag rugs with a new straw broom. Both his parents are good at supervising and finding fault. In the evening we play endless games of euchre punctuated with stories about Will's childhood that now even I can recite from memory.

This year I had the perfect excuse not to go: I had to see my property on Cook's Lake.

It wasn't an easily made decision. First, I had to negotiate with Will's mother. Then, with Bonnie. Bonnie was so anxious to see my inheritance that she'd come up with a plan: Will and I would drive up to Cook's Lake together; he would go on to his parents' cottage on Sunday when Robin and Bonnie arrived to stay with me. They would take me back to the city with them the next day.

"I'm not sure it'll work out," I protested when Bonnie began to draw up lists of the food we would need to take. "I don't even know how many bedrooms there are, if there's electricity or indoor plumbing, or even furniture."

"No problem. You don't want a cottage to be like a suburban house. We don't mind roughing it."

"But if it's too primitive, we may go straight on to Will's parents' place."

"I'm sure you'll want to stay at Cook's Lake. I mean, you can't stand your mother-in-law, right? You've been complaining for weeks about having to open up the Cairns' cottage. Robin and I will be happy to get away from the city and keep you company there. I'm dying to see your place."

How could I tell her I didn't want them to come at all, that I wanted the time alone with Will?

A phone call from Marilyn Finch seemed to provide the perfect excuse. She called that night, waking me from a dream of a white classroom, a blank test paper, a teacher we called Petey Peterson, a tyrant who paced in front of the blackboard, tapping a pointer lightly, insistently, on the open palm of his left hand as he talked on and on about logarithms and square roots. I stood beside my desk, shamed in front of all the others for my inability to answer the simplest question. They were grinning, fingers pointing because I was bleeding, blood dripping down my skirt, forming a puddle at my feet. The bell rang. And rang and rang... I knocked over the phone in my haste to answer it.

"Is this Rosalie Cairns?" It was a woman's soft drawl.

"Yes," I scrambled for my glasses and watch. Midnight.

"I'm Marilyn Finch. Your cousin. I hope I didn't wake you?"

"Marilyn! It's good of you to call."

"I should have been in touch with you earlier, I know. But my grandmother's death shattered me, just shattered me. You may not believe me, I know I haven't been to visit her for awhile because of my business, but blood's blood. She was a fine lady."

"I never even had the chance to meet her. Or attend her funeral."

"Yes, well...she's gone now," she sighed. "Roger told me you thought we should talk. And I agree. I'd love to meet you all. Now, I'm up at the lake... "

"You're here? In Canada?"

"That's where I'm calling from. The corner store, actually. Grandmother refused to have a phone at the cottage. I came up yesterday to fetch a few things, personal things I've always kept here. I do think of the lake as my place, you know."

"I feel a little awkward about this," I confessed. "I mean I never expected anything... I never knew any of the Cooks."

"Now, honey, I'm sure we can make some kind of arrangement, satisfactory to us both. You won't be living here all the time. We could share it. Why don't you come on up here to the lake on Saturday and we can make some plans?"

It wasn't her right to invite me to my own cottage, I thought. "I was coming anyway. With my husband."

"Husband? I thought maybe we could get to know each other, on our own. Family talk. Girl talk."

I considered. Will could drop me off on his way to his parents,' killing two birds with one stone. On the other hand, he would be as anxious to meet her and to see my inheritance as I was. I remembered Bonnie's plan and gave it a twist.

"Tell you what," I suggested. "My in-laws were expecting us up at their cottage on Lake of Bays this weekend. Will and I have already made plans to come to Cook's Lake tomorrow. After he's seen the place, he could go there on Sunday. How would that be?"

"All right. You'll be here by noon?"

"Yes."

"Bye, then." The phone clicked.

I immediately dialled Will. It took quite a few rings to wake him up.

"Are you all right?" were his first words when he realized who was calling.

"Marilyn just phoned."

"Marilyn who?"

"My cousin. Marilyn Finch. I told you about her. She wants to meet me and talk about sharing the cottage."

"Sharing? It belongs to you. You could rent it to her maybe, when you didn't want to go there."

"But she's my cousin. You can't rent to a cousin."

"Why not?"

"It's just not right. She's family."

"You've never met her! What kind of family are you talking about, here?"

"Maybe we'll like each other," I suggested. "She sounds like a really nice person."

"Yeah? And how often had she been to visit her own grand-mother?"

"She said business kept her away."

"Yeah." He yawned. "Don't make any decisions about the land until you meet her, Rosie. We have to see the place first."

"Get here early on Saturday, will you?"

"Early as I can."

He was at my door by nine o'clock the next morning. I greeted him with my bag packed and a box of groceries ready to carry down to the car. We hugged for a long time.

"How did Sadie like going to stay with Karen?" I tried to pull away, but he held me close.

"She wasn't too happy about the cats, but she'll be all right. It's just a weekend, after all. She'll get lots of walks, lots of treats. I wish my mother wasn't so allergic to her. She'd have loved it up north."

Our dog Sadie is a mixed breed, part Lab and part, as we joked, Irish wolfhound. Because she's so big, people who don't know her think she's dangerous. Will's mother for one. She hates the fact we gave the dog a human name and that we're quite unashamed to call her our child substitute. Sadie is a bit spoiled — she loves to jump on people to lick their faces. Especially after she's been in the bush and had a chance to roll in smelly wet mud. I wanted to make a good impression on my new cousin; I could guarantee that Sadie would have caused commotion. She was better off staying with my best friend as she's done before. I missed her, though.

Will had dressed up today for our meeting with Dr. Finch. He looked very professional in a striped cotton shirt and pale pleated pants. "Ice cream colours," I said, stepping back to get a full view. He wouldn't let go. "You look good enough to eat."

"I hope so." One hand bunched up my shirt, searching for bare skin, bra hooks.

"We've got to leave," I protested. "I told Marilyn we'd be there around lunchtime and it's at least a three-hour drive."

"But I haven't seen you all week. I have certain pressing marital issues to discuss."

When that kiss ended, I said, "We should write a book. How

to revive your marriage by living apart."

"Not totally recommended. The house is pretty empty without you in it."

My hands slid down his back, pulled him closer to me. "What will we tell Marilyn if she's prepared lunch for us and it's spoiled?"

"Traffic's heavy," he murmured into my hair.

Two hours later, and we were ready to leave at last. When the phone rang, I almost didn't answer. "Let the machine take care of it."

"You'd better see who it is," Will objected. "It might be your cousin, wondering where we are."

It wasn't.

"This is Detective Gianelli," said a deep male voice. "Do you remember me? We met at the Baker house."

"Yes, Detective. Is there any problem?"

"Not exactly," he paused. "Have you heard recently from Dr. Marilyn Finch, by any chance?"

"My cousin? As a matter of fact, yes. I'm about to go north to spend the weekend with her at the cottage."

"That's the property the old lady willed to you?"

"Yes."

"Where is that? Exactly?"

I told him how to find the cottage, and then asked, "Why do you want to know?"

"Curious. What about Roger Markham?"

"What about him?"

"Seen him recently? Possibly with your cousin?"

"I saw him yesterday morning, but I haven't met my cousin yet. That's why I'm going north. What's this all about?"

"We're following up some information about the Baker case. There's a few questions we have, and we can't seem to get hold of Dr. Finch."

"She's staying at the lake. There's no phone there."

"When you see her, will you ask her to get in touch as soon as possible?"

"Why?"

"We have a few questions."

"You're not going to tell me anything, are you?"

"Nothing to tell. Just following up."

"Are you all right, by the way? Did you have to get forty rabies shots?"

"They don't do that any more. Besides, the cats had all had their rabies shots."

"That's a relief, then."

"Yeah. You ask your cousin to call, okay?"

"Okay."

I'd barely hung up the phone when it rang again. This time it was Dufferin Ross.

"Are you going up north?" he asked.

"Yes. We're about to leave."

"Have the police been in touch with you?"

"I just had a call from Detective Gianelli. He's looking for Dr. Finch and Roger Markham. Do you know why?"

Mr. Ross sighed. "I'm afraid Roger has been up to no good."

"What do you mean?"

"He's been helping Dr. Finch to get power-of-attorney over Beatrice's estate."

"What for?"

"She claims she wanted to spare Beatrice worry over paying bills and taxes. I don't believe her."

"Why not?"

"I shouldn't say. The case is under investigation."

"What case?" I almost yelled. "You have to tell me. I'm on my way to see Dr. Finch now, and I hear that the police are looking for her, you imply that your nephew's involved. What's going on?"

"Dr. Finch is involved in a criminal procedure in the States. She needs money."

"Someone's suing her?"

"It's a little more complicated than that."

"Well? Come on, you can't just leave me hanging. I need to know who I'm dealing with."

"She was charged, along with some others, with illegally excavating and looting an archaeological site on a farm down south. There's a big market for Indian artifacts in the States; there's also enormous fines, even prison sentences, if you're convicted. Marilyn got caught on a university-sponsored dig early in the fall. Her case comes to court this summer."

"Wow." I twirled a strand of hair around my fingers, winding it tighter and tighter. "That's why she's no longer working at the university."

"Yes. I never told Beatrice the truth of the matter. It would have upset her greatly."

"Is that why Roger was helping her to get power-of-attorney? So they could sell off the property?"

"They had already had the land surveyed. Beatrice just found out about it; she was livid. When she told me, I suspected what was up."

"When did Aunt Beatrice find out?" I said.

"The week before she died, she got a letter from a real estate company making enquiries about the subdivision of the land. I was coming to see her anyway, to meet you and discuss the situation."

I thought about this for a moment. "You think Roger or Marilyn had already been there? You think one of them killed her?"

"I hate to think that." He paused. "The police have told me they have a potential witness. One of the neighbours says he saw a light on upstairs in her house..."

"I thought the upstairs had been closed up."

"It had, but she had George's papers up there. Someone has been through the desk recently."

"I wonder why."

"A copy of your birth certificate was there. And the announcement of your parents' wedding."

"Oh." I remembered Markham's insinuations about the validity of my claim to inherit the land.

"The neighbour said he saw a visitor leaving in the late afternoon, about the time she died. Couldn't tell if it was a man or a woman, but whoever it was, was in a hurry. But you know old men." Mr. Ross coughed out a laugh. "His eyesight's not too good. It could have been the grocery delivery. She had them come twice a week. Not that day, though."

"The police just let him talk," I said, remembering how Gianelli had described their "technique."

"That's right."

"So they think her death wasn't an accident?"

He didn't answer for a moment, then merely repeated his first request. "You ask Dr. Finch to call them. And if you see Roger, I wouldn't say a word to him. He's been up to some funny business, I'm afraid."

"You think he'll be up north?"

The old man sighed. "I don't know. I don't seem to know anything these days. You just take care, you hear?"

It began to rain as soon as we left the city, along with everyone else who has a cottage, wants a cottage, or knows someone with a cottage they can visit. It always rains on holiday weekends; that's the first rule of cottage life.

North of Orillia, the farmscape gave way to shield country: we drove through a granite cut, walls of glistening black and orange rock rising on either side, a stream of run-off racing along the shoulder towards a small lake that lay flat and gray below us. Dotted among the uniform dark green blanket of spruce and cedar forest that undulated over the hills were brave white flags of birch trunks, new green leaves glistening on stands of maple, poplar and scrub oak.

Small dirt roads angled off the highway, marked by posts festooned with hand lettered arrows pointing to cottages on lakes we couldn't see. Yellow signs picturing leaping deer gave way to warnings of moose crossings. In some places, for miles it seemed, a wire fence bordered the ditch, and posters tacked to trees warned away trespassers. Beaver swamps interrupted the woods, brooks rushed away under concrete bridges.

Houses had been built in clearings hacked out of the bush. Some were bungalows, hastily constructed and covered with plain white vinyl siding, set in a square of tidy lawn with per- haps a concrete deer poised, one foot raised, at the tree line. Others, half-hidden in a grove of pruned young maples, were built of rough-hewn logs, square and squat, one high dormer window centred over a bright red door.

Most of the driveways were empty, though lights shone in one or two houses, in kitchens, I bet silently to myself. I imag- ined a young woman wearing a pale green tracksuit, her hair caught back in a neat ponytail. She eases herself down on a wooden rocker, a steaming cup cradled in her hands. The breakfast dishes are in the drainer, a yeasty smell fills the house from the bread she's just put in the oven. She leans her head back, closes her eyes. A clock ticks. In another room, a baby murmurs in its sleep. Her eyes flick open, then slowly fall again. A cat pads into the room, considers her for a moment, jumps into her lap. The tea spills.

I shook myself free of the dream; the young woman, the blue and white kitchen, and the cat faded away. I stifled a yawn with a cough.

"You okay?" Will asked. He leaned forward over the wheel, peering through the half moons made by the windshield wipers at the tail-lights of the car in front.

"Just dozing."

"Pretty heavy doze. You've been snoring for the last fifty miles."

"I have not."

"Heavy breathing then. Good dream?"

"No." I rooted through my bag hoping that I'd had the sense to pack some fruit juice, perhaps an apple. I like to think I'm an organized sort of person. I had spent long enough packing for this trip at any rate, trying on clothes, trying to decide what would be appropriate wear for a weekend with my cousin.

But I hadn't packed anything to drink. "Could we stop, please? I'm dying of thirst."

"There must be a gas station pretty soon. There's supposed to be one near the road to the cottage."

The map Mr. Ross gave me had directions written in meticulous script and coloured pencil marks for water and trees. A little box represented the country store at the corner where we were to turn off the highway. A dotted line indicated the dirt road which wound for a couple of miles down from the highway to the shore where it passed over a bridge (two black parallel lines over a wavering blue streak) and ended at a large X. The cottage itself was on the river, separated from the lake by a stretch of dense marsh, my grandfather's bird sanctuary. Access to the beach — a long thin curve of brown between the blue of the bay and the thick green line of bush — was by canoe up the river and around a point of reeds. If this rain kept up all weekend, I doubted I would ever get that far.

"Dreaming again?"

"What?"

"There's a gas station up ahead, see the lights? Want to stop? We're almost there."

"I really need something to drink. My mouth feels full of cotton batten."

The car tires crunched on gravel and the engine protested as Will downshifted to a stop. A German shepherd appeared at the open bay of the empty double garage, spotlit in our car headlights. It sat just on the edge of shelter, facing us. In the sudden silence when Will turned off the motor, we listened to the rain drum on the roof and the steady swish of traffic passing by.

"*Downtown Cook's Lake,*" Will read the letters painted in faded red script on the false front of the store. "I wonder where uptown is. Talk about hyperbole — or hope."

"It's meant to be a joke."

"The place sure doesn't look like much."

The false front obscured the slope of the roof, but the building, though just one storey, obviously contained living quarters as well as the shop. Smoke curled from a metal chimney that snaked up a wall whose white vinyl siding was stained yellow and black from years of creosote build-up and ash. On the concrete stoop to one side of the screen door were a three-legged stool and a rusting oil drum used as a garbage pail; above it, a bulletin board sagged with layers of notices tacked over each other and around its frame. On the other side of the door was a pay telephone shielded in blue plastic.

I took a deep breath, pushed open the car door, slammed it behind me and ran for the ramp that led to the entrance. The screen opened into an interior so dark that I thought at first the place was empty. One fluorescent tube buzzed on the high ceiling. I could hear television applause, the high-pitched racing commentary of a game show host from somewhere in the darkness behind the counter.

This counter was a wood-framed showcase, its shelves packed with chocolate bars and jars of the penny candy I hadn't seen since grade school. A computer cash register looked incongruous beside the boxes of rope licorice and piles of newspapers that shared the top with a lottery board. A carousel of paperback thrillers and romances was propped between one of its corners and a wall of shelves filled with canned soup, boxes of instant meals, bottles of household cleaners and a pile of mousetraps. A refrigerator unit hummed to my right, its dim light reflecting bags of milk and neat rows of soft drinks. Beside it, a red warning flashed on the lid of a giant chest freezer.

Under the high windows that fronted the store were more shelves, these lined with fishing rods and nets, baskets of lures, boxes of reels, rolls of line. A row of plaques and notices in bright neon colours were tacked above the door: *Fishing Licences Available; Beware Of Dog; Sale By Owner; The Fisherman's Prayer.* From hooks on the ceiling hung sweatshirts printed with wild animals and beer slogans; a cascade of baseball caps and brilliant orange hunting hats obscured a glass case on the other side of the counter. I thought I saw a rifle inside, boxes of shells. As I moved forward to get a better look, something stirred in the shadows of the hall.

"Help you?"

It was more a grunt than a question. I blinked as light filled the store, bank after bank of fluorescents turning on. The TV went silent. A man stood framed against the black rectangle of the hall. A boy actually, trying to disguise his age by the aggressiveness of his stance, groin in tight blue jeans thrust forward, bare tattooed arms crossed over the picture on his black cropped sweatshirt. He couldn't be more than sixteen or seventeen: there was no sign of moustache or beard on the deeply tanned skin of his face. He wore his long black hair gelled straight back from his forehead and gathered into a pony tail. A cigarette smoked between his lips. Elvis, I thought. James Dean.

"Have you got soda water? Juice?"

He pointed to the fridge.

"Wet weather, isn't it?" I forged on. Other than milk and a few tall cartons of orange juice, the shelves were stocked with different brands and flavours of pop, artificially sweetened and over-carbonated. I finally settled on root beer and turned back to the boy.

He slouched against the hall doorframe. I could feel him staring, but when I turned, his eyes slid away to his own feet. His mouth was pursed around the cigarette, his full lips twisted in a smile as if he'd judged and found me wanting, too old and too ordinary to be interesting. My hair had frizzed with the damp into a mess of brown curls that tumbled down over the shoulders of the oversize neon pink T-shirt I wore over black denim jeans. It was too early in the year for a tan and, as I never wore make-up, I knew how pale my face must look in this harsh light, how my eyes were magnified by the thick lenses I had to wear.

I'm forty years old, I told myself. I'm too old for this. And he's much too young. But I could feel myself flush, hot blood burning my cheeks. I banged the can on the counter. "How much?"

"Dollar." He straightened up, flexing his shoulders to draw attention to the muscles of his upper arms. A snarling cougar leaped across his chest. He leaned forward and I stepped back, but he was only reaching for an ashtray. He stubbed out his cigarette, grinding the tip into the bed of ashes and butts. I rooted in my wallet for a loonie. He held out his palm for my money, the middle finger curled in. I put the coin on the counter.

"How close is the road to Cook's Lake?"

"Cook's Lake?" he repeated. He glanced down the dark hall. I thought I heard someone moving there, a strange whispering rush, but could see nothing in the gloom. "You visiting there?"

I nodded.

"You want the Indian Point cottages? You missed the road; you gotta go back down the highway about five miles. Its the Fifth Line you want; you'll see the sign. Road's not paved, but the grader's been through this week."

"Actually, I'm going to the Cook cottage. It's on a private road, I think. Do you know it?"

"You got business with that woman?" a new voice interrupted. The same soft whisper announced a wheelchair which now slid into view. Its occupant was an old man, older even than Mr. Ross. His legs and feet were entirely wrapped and bound in a frayed multi-coloured quilt. His hands were folded on his lap, a white handkerchief pressed between long and perfectly manicured fingers. The deep red stone on his ring glowed. He wore a suit jacket, a white shirt with high starched collar, a thin blue tie. One lock of thick gray hair fell carefully over his high forehead, the combed eyebrows, the clear and steady deep blue eyes. The wrinkles around these eyes and at the corner of his full lips only added character to a face sculpted with high cheekbones, square chin.

"Do you mean Marilyn Finch? She's my cousin."

"Cousin?" The old man said, his voice breathy and high. "You're George Cook's granddaughter? Beatrice found you after all."

"You knew my aunt?"

His laugh was the creaking of skeletal doors, dry and without amusement. "Oh, yes. I knew her. And your grandfather too. Stole my land, they did. It doesn't belong to them, or you. I worked it. It's mine, by right of that, if nothing else."

The boy put his hand on the old man's shoulder. "Take it easy, Grandad," he cautioned. He glanced at me. "It's an old story."

"You must be a McDonnel," I stepped forward eagerly. "I'm pleased to meet you. We're related somehow: my name's Rosie Cairns now, but my father was George Cook."

"Cooks," he snorted. "Never had time for them folk. Thought they were too good for the working man, they did." He pushed the chair back a bit and peered up at me. "Not your fault, though. I guess." He nodded at the younger man. "He's your second cousin, twice removed — Hank McDonnel. And I'm Henry McDonnel, his grandfather, your great-uncle."

When we shook hands, Hank held on too long and squeezed too tightly. Whatever message he was trying to convey, I didn't want to receive it. I spoke only to the old man. "As far as I know, the land belonged to my great-aunt, and she willed it to me."

"Thieving bastards. Just because the Cooks had money and paid the taxes don't give them the right to the land."

"They had title too," I pointed out.

"Title," he snorted. "You're a modern woman, one of them libbers, I bet. What do you think of an old man wouldn't let his daughter and her husband inherit the property, even though they stayed in the big house with him when her brother left for the city. Eh? What do you think of that, then?"

I shrugged uneasily.

The old man coughed. "The son makes money burying folks and his son comes back up here, bold as brass, wants to build a summer home on the lake. Summer home! I been working that land since I was fourteen years old. Fourteen. And not one holiday then or since."

"She doesn't want a whole life history," Hank interrupted.

"Yes, I do," I said. "I don't know any of this. Is this your store?"

"Oh, aye. Farming don't pay. Specially when the land's not in your name. I had an accident," he gestured at his legs. "Couldn't work any more. My son's dead." He shrugged his grandson's hand off his shoulder. "Just him and me now."

"I'm sorry," I said.

He glared at me. "That land's mine because I worked it, because of the blood it took from me. No one's got the right to take it away, not you, not that fancy woman from the States. Divide it all up for a bunch of city slickers to come play on. Waste of good land. It's a sin." His voice rose to a shout.

"Take it easy, Grandad," Hank repeated. "Remember what the doctor said about your blood pressure."

"Doctors," the old man snapped. "What do they know? My time'll come when my time comes. And not soon enough, I say. When a man's land is taken away from him, for some slip of a girl he doesn't even know."

The car horn blared. We all jumped.

"Someone waiting for you?" Hank asked me.

"My husband."

"You're married? You got kids?"

I shook my head.

"A grief and a blessing," the old man muttered. "I know I sometimes wonder what use children are supposed to be. Comfort in my old age. Hah."

"Yes," I said. "Well, I have to get going. I haven't even been to the cottage yet. I'm sorry about what happened in the past, but it's not my fault, and the lawyer tells me the land's mine legally."

"Legal," the old man snorted. "Law belongs to who has the most money. I'm talking moral here. I'm talking about what's right."

"I don't know," I said. "Beatrice left the land to me and that's all I know about it."

"Outsider. Know-nothing." He turned his wheelchair

around and disappeared into the darkness of the hall. A moment later, the television switched on in a roar of laughter.

Hank wiped his hand across his mouth and turned away as if to follow his grandfather back indoors. I thought that if he'd been chewing tobacco, he would have taken this moment to spit. He had that air about him.

"What was that all about?" I asked him.

Hank shrugged. "Old man gets upset easy these days. That Beatrice, she treated him like dirt. Always promised she'd do right by him, then turns around and gives the land to a stranger. Beg your pardon, but there you are. Makes him a bit hot."

"It's not my fault. I never even knew my father, or any of his family." The old hurt welled up again, my mother huddled on a kitchen chair, clutching herself, rocking back and forth, cursing his name over and over. I sighed. "I didn't ask for the land. Apparently Beatrice wanted me to have it."

The car horn blared a second time.

"You been married long?" Hank asked.

"Twenty years." I expected his whistle of disbelief and added the joke I always used. "I was a teen-age bride, married for money. Student loans, actually. We got married in our last year at university."

"Kind of boring, isn't it? Twenty years with the same old man?"

"It's not boring and he's not old."

"No?" His tongue ran around his lips. "Maybe you want to come by sometime when you're up here on your own. You going to be up here much?"

"I don't know." I opened the door.

"Say hi to my old cuz, Marilyn, will you? Tell her she ought to drop by, I got some bones to pick with her." He giggled. "We're kissing cousins, you know. You know what that means?"

"I don't think I want to know."

"It's all in the family," he grinned. "So to speak."

The door slammed behind me. I took a deep breath, preparing to run through the rain.

Hank's voice came through the screen, so close I could feel his breath hot on the back of my neck. "Just maybe I'll drop by," he added. "One of these days — or nights."

SEVEN

"What took so long?" Will asked.

"More relatives." I groped for the box of tissues we keep in the car. There were only a couple left, enough to wipe the wetness from my glasses.

"Cousins or something?"

"Something is right. Henry McDonnel and his grandson Hank. Second cousins twice removed. Do you have any idea what that means?"

"My mother would know."

"Goes back generations anyway. And so does the grudge. Apparently they feel the land belongs to them." I sighed. "I wish Aunt Beatrice had decided to keep her guilt to herself. Or died sooner."

"Rosie! That doesn't sound like you."

"Not the dying part. But this land business has been one big headache. First Roger Markham and the litigious Dr. Finch. Now the McDonnels." I shivered. "Hank gives me the creeps."

"Why?" Will eased the car to the edge of the parking lot and waited for a break in the traffic. The rain was letting up.

"It's his attitude. He's just a kid, but I swear he thinks he's Elvis come back from the dead. All tight jeans and cigarettes. He implied that he and Marilyn were rather close. Kissing cousins, he said."

"Isn't he kind of young for her?"

"You'd think so. She's my age and he looks like he's barely in his teens. She'd be robbing the cradle."

"He must have been putting you on."

"Teasing? Maybe. I keep thinking about what Robin says all the time."

"What's that?"

"You can pick your friends, but not your family."

Will laughed. "Or your family picks you. You realize that you're all at the end of the line, you, Marilyn and Hank."

"Unless there's a Mrs. Hank in the offing. He's awfully young, though."

"We weren't exactly elderly when we got together," Will teased.

"It's not the same. Besides, he didn't look married."

"Not haggard and hen-pecked like me?"

I punched him softly on the shoulder. "Cut it out. That's not what I meant. He's only a boy."

"So were they surprised to meet you?"

"Hard to tell. They weren't exactly overjoyed. I hope Marilyn's a bit more welcoming than that."

"We could always forget about going there and go straight to my parents' cottage."

"What are you so worried about?"

He shrugged. "I don't know. The whole set up seems odd. Why wouldn't she want me to stay too?"

"Perhaps she feels she'd be more comfortable with just me by myself."

"Maybe she's got something else in mind. Remember what Wilson implied about her and Markham, that they're up to something."

"I don't believe she would have anything to do with her grandmother's death. Markham, maybe. But he's in the city."

"She needs money."

"Everyone needs money. Besides, too many people know I'm going to be there alone with her. She wouldn't dare try anything."

"You'll be careful, won't you?"

I put one hand on my heart and held the other up. "I promise on my honour not to go in the woods alone. Or out in a tippy canoe with a maniac. Or eat anything she's not eating."

Will grinned. "And if the wolf comes to the door?"

"He can huff and puff, but I won't let him in."

Will ran his fingers back through his hair. He was graying at the temples and I sometimes teased him by counting the white strands that peppered his beard. He had grown it when his business began to take off a couple of years ago. The beard looked distinguished then, but now I thought it made him look too old, much older than his forty-two years. He was stubborn about it, preferring the luxury of not shaving to my vanity.

A break had finally come in the traffic. With a spray of gravel, we crossed the highway and bounced over a cattle grid. Although the McDonnels were no longer farming the land, the papers from my aunt included a lease arrangement with the neighbouring farmer that allowed him to graze cattle on the property.

The road was little more than a laneway, pitted with muddy holes and tufted with grass. Tree branches met overhead so that we seemed to be in a long green tunnel that twisted and slid down through the hills. In the tangled branches of one such group I recognized the remains of an apple orchard. A snake fence disappeared into the bush and a pile of rocks in a field choked with alder and sumac indicated where a pasture had once been cleared. In another open space, a small herd of cows grazed around the stone foundations of a boarded-up house.

"That must have been quite some place at one time," Will said. He idled to a stop. One by one, the cows raised their heads to turn towards us, staring. A calf tottered towards the road, then turned to scamper, tail high, behind the building.

It was a big house, two full stories and an attic under the peaked roof. The windows on the first floor and the front door had been boarded shut; the glass in most of the others was missing, shot out by boys with BB guns or victims of the weather. A verandah that ran around two sides of the house had collapsed in a pile of gray wood and shingles, half buried in a tangle of rose bushes that sent sprays of new green up the faded red brick walls. A rotting chimney leaned over a hole in the roof.

"The proverbial haunted house," I said.

"Do you suppose it was the Cook family home?"

"Must be. Old Henry said they lived in the big house. When do you think it was built?"

"Late Victorian era. Look at the masonry, the use of that yellow brick as decoration on the corners and around the doors and windows. And you can still see the pattern of coloured shingles on the roof. Someone spent a lot of money to build this place."

"I wonder when it was abandoned."

"Years ago. It's too bad. They must have just packed up and left it to rot."

"Revenge on the Cooks for taking the land back," I said.

I popped open the can of root beer and took a long swallow. When I was a kid, the only two fast food outlets in our suburb were the A & W and Red Barn, both hamburger joints. After football games, we headed for the A & W where girls only slightly older than us, girls who had finished grade twelve or who had dropped out as soon as they turned sixteen, brought trays of burgers and root beer in thick glass mugs out to the cars parked in tidy rows. I still had one of those mugs. We didn't call it shoplifting or stealing in those days, but "liberating."

"Can I have some?" Will held out his hand and I passed him the can. He grimaced. "How can you drink this stuff?"

"It used to taste a lot better. And there wasn't much choice."

He handed it back. "I guess we'd better get a move on. I hope this road doesn't get any worse. Should have brought the truck."

We crested a rise. The sun broke in a thick red band through the gray blanket of clouds and drew silver streaks across the surface of a wide inlet, enclosed on both sides by forested hills and protected from the rougher waters of the open lake by a chain of low islands. The lake was so long that we couldn't see the cottages at its other end.

"That must be the marsh." I pointed to a wide strip of green which from this distance looked like a lush meadow bordering the white beach.

Will started driving slowly down the incline. "Look." He pointed to a wooden stake painted orange and planted at the roadside. "Survey posts."

I squinted into the field and made out another, farther down towards the water. "They must have had the whole farm divided up for tier development."

"Wouldn't there be environmental restrictions on such a large amount of building so close to the lake?"

"This is a working farm up here. Would pesticide run-off be any worse than septic systems?"

"They wouldn't have had to worry about any environmental issues if they'd sold it years ago. They could have carved it up however the fancy took them."

"My grandfather always insisted that the land was to go to the province if the family didn't want it. He wanted to save the marshes for a bird sanctuary. He hated hunters and speed-boats."

"But he gave title to Beatrice. She could have sold it."

"She didn't seem to care much for money. You know, the last time I talked to him, Mr. Ross implied she might have left the land to me out of spite."

"What do you mean?"

"Apparently, she was fed up with Marilyn. Probably because of the power-of-attorney business. And maybe she suspected that Markham had designs on the land, and since he and Marilyn seemed to be rather close..."

"Do you think she knew about the law suit and Marilyn's need for money?"

"Hard to say. She must have been plenty upset to disinherit her own granddaughter in favour of a stranger, though. It's a wonder Marilyn wants to have anything to do with me at all. She probably will try to get me to sell, thinking I don't know that she's already had the place surveyed."

"Even a modest division of this land along the water would be worth a lot of money."

"Half a million is what they offered."

"Peanuts." Will slowed to another stop before a wooden bridge that spanned a swiftly running creek. "You think it's safe?" he asked.

"I'll check it."

When I got out, I could smell the marsh, a rich ooze that permeated the air. A stiff breeze rattled the little leaves. Water tumbled white over rocks in the riverbed which was only a few yards wide; its banks were steep grass-covered inclines. A robin repeated its rain song over and over. A red-winged blackbird trilled.

The bridge consisted of wide planks laid over a simple trestle. They seemed firm underfoot. It was narrow and without guard rails: only one car could pass over at a time. I waved to Will from the far side. He gingerly crossed, the boards rattling beneath the wheels.

The river veered away from the road. After a few hundred yards, I had to get out of the car again, this time to open a gate that protected the cottage lot from the cows. It was hooked shut by a chain looped over the fence post, a padlock lying on the ground beneath it. I picked it up. It had been broken, the hoop completely torn from the body of the lock.

"Look at this." I handed it through the window to Will.

"Probably rusted shut." He turned it over in his hands. "You can see where someone's tried to use a key, it's all scratched up. Probably just took a crowbar to it in frustration."

I swung the gate shut and fastened the chain again. "The cottage can't be far now."

The driveway took us through a wood lot before widening in a circle that had once been gravelled. We parked under a huge basswood tree beside another car covered with a pale green tarpaulin.

Into the silence left by the ticking of the engine as it cooled poured birdsong, the rush of wind through new leaves. The bush had been barely cleared to make room for the driveway and the cottage. Giant white pines that had grown here since long before settlement and lumbering tamed the land circled the clearing which was dotted with maples, birch and poplar. Undergrowth had been cut back enough to let the spring woodland flowers bloom; beds of trilliums and dogtooth violets splashed colour against the floor of matted leaves and pine needles. There was no lawn, only a few patches of wild grass struggling to gain a foothold between granite outcroppings and muddy hollows.

A path of beaten earth, marked here and there by coloured quartz rocks, led up to the cottage which was perched on the top of a knoll. It was a long, low, log structure with a tin roof dominated by a wide fieldstone chimney, capped by a chicken wire net. Two of the huge pines bracketed a screened porch that extended out over a rock ledge at one end; a third pine pressed against the far wall, a black silent sentinel. The windows were dark. High overhead, branches rubbed against each other, a sawing, sighing whine.

I opened the screen and knocked on the wood door. "Marilyn?" I called. "Dr. Finch? It's Rosie Cairns here. Marilyn?"

Two blue jays swooped through the clearing, quarrelling as they disappeared into the bush.

"No one home?" Will asked, as he lowered the sack of groceries he'd carried up from the car on to the top step.

I tried the door but it was bolted shut. "I guess she got tired of waiting." The two windows on either side of the door were heavily curtained. I stood on tiptoe, but couldn't see in.

"You didn't forget the key?"

"Of course not, but there's no lock here. It must fit a door around on the other side."

"Maybe she's outside and didn't hear us drive up."

We circled the screened porch, watching for roots that arched out of the moss and dead leaves. The cottage was built on pilings a foot or so off the ground; rotting latticework had once kept out animals but we could see definite signs where something — raccoon or porcupine — had tunnelled in.

"Sadie would love this," Will murmured.

"I couldn't bring her, not the first time. What if Marilyn is allergic or hates dogs? It would have been too difficult. Sadie is just too big to be ignored."

The front of the cottage faced an opening in the trees that looked down a long hill to a wide brown pool through which the river current was hurrying a raft of branches and leaves. A red canoe was turned upside down on a narrow dock which hugged the steep bank of the near shore while the other side was smothered in bullrushes. From this height, we could see over the waving reeds to a line of open water. Red-winged blackbirds trilled over and over as swallows flocked in whirling masses over the marsh. The air sang with mosquitoes.

"Black flies," Will batted the cloud of insects that swarmed around his ears. "I hope we can get in before we get eaten alive."

Two big picture windows filled the front wall and looked

out towards the distant bay. I pulled open the screen door and tried the latch of the wooden door behind it. It didn't budge. The lock above it was shiny and new; my key didn't fit there either.

Will tried banging on the door and shouting. The birds fell silent for a moment but took up their chatter once he subsided. "Are you sure she was expecting us today?"

"Yes. We're a bit late, but still it's kind of odd. I wonder when the locks were changed."

I leaned over the railing of the stoop and peered inside. A big open room had a kitchen with woodstove and long harvest table at one end and a brown tweed sofa with matching easy chairs facing the wide fireplace at the other. A glass door, shut tight, opened onto the verandah. The cottage had been divided in half down its length. Directly in front of me across the space dividing the living and eating areas a hall led to the back door; the rooms on either side must be bedrooms.

Will slapped at the back of his neck. "I can't stand this any longer. Let's get out of here."

We continued around the cottage. Will hurried back down to the car. I looked at the small windows again. Behind the screen of one, the casement had been propped open. Beside a small woodpile next to the path was a stump used for a chopping block. I rolled it over to the house; by standing on it, my head was almost level to the bottom of the window. I managed to poke a thin-edged twig between the screen's frame and the window moulding, working it up and down until I hit a hook. Leaving the twig lodged there, I searched around for something a bit sturdier. A small lean-to shed had been left unlocked; inside, on a shelf laden with rolls of screen, buckets, a rusted hibachi, and jars crammed with screws and nails was a basket of old tools, including a screwdriver. I used it to force the hook out of its socket. The screen swung free.

"Let me help." Will took my place on the stump and pushed upwards at the window. Nothing happened. He took the screwdriver and pounded its handle all around the frame and pushed again. The wood screamed; the window slid slowly upward.

"Who's going in?" I stood on tiptoe, pushed aside the heavy curtain material, and peered into the gloom of the bedroom.

In front of me was an antique bed with a high, elaborately carved headboard. It was unmade: sheets, blankets and a white candlewick bedspread had been dumped in an untidy pile in its middle. On top was an open suitcase, its contents tumbled about as if its owner couldn't decide what to wear and had pulled everything out and stuffed them back in without paying attention. Wedged in the corner beside the closed door was an enormous wardrobe whose full-length mirror sent me a picture of my face pitted and wavery with age. A tall narrow dresser served as a bedside table; on it perched a lamp in the shape of a leaping trout, the bare bulb emerging from its gaping mouth. A row of hooks on the back of the door was empty. I called for Marilyn again, and was greeted with the faint skittering of some small creature across the roof.

"I don't think I'd fit," Will strained to push the window up further, but the frame had swollen through too many unpainted winters and would budge no farther. "As soon as you get in, come and open the door."

"Don't worry, I don't plan to waste any time."

I remembered seeing a wheelbarrow in the shed and went back for it. It wobbled on its shaft but I managed to drag it under the window. I turned it upside down and stood on it to get some leverage. Will tried to help but when he released his grip on the window it began to slide back down. There was only room to go in head first. I got both hands on the sill and pushed with both feet. The wheelbarrow toppled but I was halfway in, in a cloud of dust and the sound of ripping fabric as the curtain came with me. I reached down to touch the floor and wriggled my hips, crab-walking across a rag rug until my legs slipped in. Both knees thudded down hard. I rolled over, sat up, rubbed at the pain. They would be bruised tomorrow.

"You okay?"

"Yeah. You can let the window go." It crashed down behind me.

The bedroom door opened into a narrow hall. Directly across was a second bedroom containing a set of bunk beds built into the wall, another small dresser, and a bookshelf crammed with tattered paperbacks and thin boxes that must be games and jigsaw puzzles. Mattresses were rolled at the foot of both beds, an empty light socket hung from the ceiling.

Will banged on the back door. It was bolted at floor and ceiling with long iron rods that inched stiffly out of their sockets.

"Damn bugs." He showed me a smear of blood across his cheek.

"Did you put the screen back on?"

"As well as I could. I'll have to fix it from inside. Your cousin will understand. She wouldn't expect us to wait outside in the dark."

It was getting dark, too quickly for evening. Clouds rolled in from the bay and a jagged fork of lightning split the sky. Great flocks of birds were flying into the marshes, and even inside we could hear the tremendous clatter of their nesting rites.

I looked around the cottage anxiously. "I guess this is the right place? We haven't broken into a stranger's?"

Will picked up a book lying open and face down on the coffee table in front of the fireplace. "It's got her name in it," he said. He showed me the bookplate carefully glued inside the front cover. "This is the cottage, all right."

"Where do you think she is?"

On the harvest table were the remains of breakfast: a coffee mug and a plate of crumbs. A fly was trapped on the sticky lid of an open jar of strawberry jam which swarmed with ants. A small carton of cream breathed sourness into the close air of the room. Two baguettes wrapped in plastic film stuck out of a paper bag on the counter by the sink. I dumped the bread and, picking up the jam jar with two fingers, dropped it in. The lid went in too, and the crumbs. I hate bugs.

"Looks like she left in a hurry." Will circled the room switching on lamps. A motor whirred and a fan began to revolve high up among the exposed rafters that criss-crossed the ceiling. We both looked up into the shadows. After a moment, he flicked it off.

"She didn't forget to lock up." I crossed over to the small fridge that rumbled away to itself in a corner of the kitchen. Inside were two bottles of Perrier, two bottles of French wine, a six pack of Heineken beer, half a pound of unsalted butter in foil wrapping, a variety of cheeses, and a five-pound box of chocolates.

"Maybe she went shopping."

"Leaving her breakfast on the table? And how did she go? Whose car is out there?"

"Maybe Markham came to get her."

"Why?"

"To talk about how they were going to get you to sell your land."

"It's beautiful here." I stared out the glass door at the lake. The birds had fallen silent except for the last late seagulls who came in squawking low over the reeds. The lake was a pewter reflection of the sky.

Thunder shook the cottage.

"We'd better bring the rest of the stuff in. Good thing you brought some food after all."

Lights flickered and the fridge stuttered to a momentary stop before its grumbling began again. Rain spattered the picture window.

"A fine welcome for the prodigal." I emptied the cold coffee down the drain and followed Will out the door.

EIGHT

A well-worn path led through a screen of bushes to an out-house. Someone had had a lot of fun building it. A mock Athenian arch topped the door which was flanked by scrolled pillars. Inside three steps led up to the throne: with the door open, you could look through a gap in the trees to the lake. Colour photographs of birds and small mammals, cut from nature magazines, papered the walls. Toilet paper was kept safe from mice in a metal breadbox. A screened crescent moon in the back wall let in fresh air.

The shower was over; the dark rustled with animals under the trees and the croaking of frogs, millions of them it seemed, ranging from the hollow bass of bullfrogs to the shrill cheeping of tree frogs. I almost preferred the steady hum of traffic to their noise.

Will was putting the last dish back on the shelf above the sink when I came in. "Great chili," he said. "But you've got enough left over to last a week."

"I asked Bonnie's advice. She said you should always take chili to the cottage, it's the perfect food."

"Goes with the beer, I guess. Want another one?"

"Sure. I'll see if I can get a fire started."

Sticks and twigs had been arranged tent fashion in the fire-place. I crumpled up some paper from the pile of old newspa-pers in a magazine rack on one side of the hearth and added some long pine cones from the wicker basket beside it. The fireplace was deep and black with years of smoke. Built of rough cut fieldstone, it occupied most of the north wall of the cottage. On its mantel, a thick ledge of smoothed rock, was a collection of found objects: driftwood in the shape of a loon, a flaking decoy duck, a collection of keys in a ceramic ashtray, an old Mason jar filled with odd shaped pebbles and shells. Inside the chimney was a long iron hook; the cauldron it was used to support sat on the stone hearth, a fat squat pot, perfect for witches.

The paper caught quickly and soon the kindling crackled and the tent collapsed. I added some larger logs from the stack between the chimney and the outer wall, put the three-sided screen in front of the blaze and joined Will on the couch. It was a typical pull-out sofa bed in a scratchy brown tweed. A thick afghan blanket and soft down pillows made it more comfortable.

"This is more like it," he said. He handed me a cold bottle of beer, and stretched out, his feet on the coffee table, one arm around my shoulder, pulling me closer. "I'm glad your cousin isn't here."

"She's likely to return any minute now. It's pretty late."

He kissed me. We kissed for a long time. The fire collapsed on itself with a puff of smoke and sparks. I pulled only slightly away.

"Maybe we should get the beds arranged."

"Beds? Plural?"

"We can't sleep in Marilyn's bed. What if she gets back in the night? We'll have to use the bunks."

"I doubt she'll be coming back now. Anyway, we could leave her a note. Pin it to the bedroom door."

"I'm worried." I stood up and faced the windows. Rain streaked my reflection. "She knew we were coming, she wouldn't have left unless there was some kind of emergency."

"Since we were so late, she may have thought you'd chickened out of meeting with her, so decided to go into town with a friend. It's early, only ten o'clock. She may be on her way back now."

"If she went out, she would have phoned me. I left a message for her on my machine to say we were on our way. I have a feeling that something has happened to her. Remember Gianelli said they hadn't been able to get hold of her?"

"What do you want to do about it?"

"There was a pay phone outside the store. We could call the police and see if she was in an accident."

"She's probably having dinner in town with Markham. Besides, I don't relish driving up that road in this weather."

"I'll go."

"No. You should stay here in case she gets back before I do."

Lightning lit the marsh. In the peculiar white flash, the bullrushes looked like tiny little heads bobbing in unison.

"She could be with the police now, you know," Will continued. "She and Markham both."

"You'd think she'd have left a note."

"She probably expected to be back before we got here."

Thunder crashed and rumbled. My mother used to soothe my fears of storms by telling me the sound was God moving His furniture around heaven. We made a game of guessing where He put His throne. Rain pummelled the roof.

"Let's see how bad it is, before we decide to drive anywhere," Will suggested.

There was a switch by the back door which turned on an outdoor flood. The light from its dim yellow bulb was swallowed by the shadows under the great pines and illuminated only a semi-circle of sodden grass, puddles on the path, the unremitting sheets of rain. Other than its hissing passage through the leaves and the ceaseless shrill of frogs, the night was silent.

"I'm so glad we're not camping," Will murmured. He stood behind me, his arms circling my waist, his voice muffled by my hair. I shook him loose.

"Do you hear anyone coming? See anything?"

"No to both. I can barely see the driveway." He leaned over my shoulder, squinting through the rain. "Just our car and Marilyn's. That tarp is a good idea. I'll have to suggest it to my father tomorrow. He's always complaining about how dirty his car gets sitting outside under the trees."

"Listen."

Thunder grumbled over the lake and a stray breeze

splashed a handful of rain against the screen. We ducked back indoors.

"Nothing out there but the birds and beasts," Will said.

"I was hoping we'd hear Marilyn coming back." I shivered. "You're going to have to go up to the highway and phone the police and the local hospital. There's one in Minden, I think."

"If I must, I must." Will rolled his eyes. "But I left my raincoat in the car. Do you suppose there might be an umbrella or something in here?"

"I'll check the wardrobe in Marilyn's bedroom. You could see if there's anything in the pantry or the porch."

There was no ceiling fixture in Marilyn's room. The wardrobe so filled the wall beside the door that it bumped before it was open halfway. I remembered the trout lamp on the bedside table and with the little light that leaked in from the hall, edged my way across the floor towards it. The rag rug tripped me. I fell, pulling the bedspread down as well. The suitcase came with it, hitting me sharply on the shoulder before spilling its contents all over the floor. I cursed. Will came running.

"What happened?"

"Banged my stupid knee again." I crawled over to turn on the lamp. "Oh, what a mess."

Clothes had spewed across the room, a colourful jumble of silk and cotton. Tubes of make-up, toothpaste, deodorant and other personal items dotted the floor. On hands and knees, I began to pick them up. Will gathered the bedspread off the floor, carefully dumping the rest of the clothes beside the open case.

"Oh oh," he said. I looked up. He was about to make up the bed and had lifted the sheets and blanket to straighten them. He was staring down at the mattress under the tent of lifted linen. I craned to see what he was looking at. Spots on the bottom sheet. Rust red ovals smeared in streaks. Blood.

Will dropped the sheets. I sank back down on my haunches, staring up at him. The light flickered and a crack of thunder made us both jump. I put my hand on the edge of the mattress and stood. We still hadn't spoken. I hesitated a moment before pulling the sheets back again. I touched one of the stains. It was dry.

"Maybe her period started in the night? She had to go into town to get some Tampax, or something?" My voice even to me sounded unnaturally high.

Will shook himself free of the wall on which he was leaning. "That's probably it. There's not all that much of it."

"And it's in the middle of the bed. If she'd been, well, shot, you'd think there'd be more blood."

"That's what you'd think. I wish to hell she'd get back here."

"Maybe she and Markham had a fight about selling the land. She changed her mind. And it got out of hand. And he's had to take her into town to the hospital. Maybe she's filed a complaint against him and she's at the police station right now."

"Maybe you read too many detective stories. There's probably a simple explanation. Her period started or she had a nosebleed."

"In the middle of the bed? You think she was hiding under the covers?"

"Why ask me? She's your cousin."

After a moment, I let the sheet drop. "I think I'll come with you when you go to phone. The McDonnels might still be up and can tell us if she had another visitor or if they saw her leave."

"Good idea. Let's go."

"I'll just pick up the rest of this stuff." I knelt down to cram the underwear and shirts back into the case, managing in my hurry to knock a shampoo bottle under the bed. I was about to reach under after it when my muscles froze.

"Did you look under the bed?" I asked Will. He was hanging clothes on the hooks.

"When?"

"When you were looking for an umbrella."

"You were the one who came in here."

"True." I sat back on my heels and looked at the darkness under the bed. "You don't suppose..."

"That there's a body under there? No."

"You look then."

"All right." He knelt down beside me and, pushing aside the overhanging blankets, peered in. "There is something under there."

"What?" I grabbed his arm.

"Let go, that hurts." He reached in. "It's just a box."

"Pull it out."

"What if it's a coffin?"

"Ha, ha. Very funny."

"It's heavy. You'll have to give me a hand."

We both lay flat on the floor and pushed ourselves halfway under the bed.

I sneezed. "It's dusty. Marilyn's not much of a housekeeper."

"Have you got your end?"

"Yep. Ready?"

We backed out pulling the box with us. It was one of those metal chests people used to use when they travelled by sea, a steamer trunk I think they're called. Its blue paint was dented and scratched but it was locked with a shiny new padlock.

"It's probably sheets and blankets," I said. "Your mother is always saying she's going to get a trunk like this for linen storage at their cottage. It keeps the mice out."

Will rubbed his shoulder. "It's pretty heavy for blankets."

"I wonder if one of those keys on the mantel would fit the lock?"

"The Holmes theory? The best hiding place is no hiding place at all?"

"She'd have no reason to hide the key if it's just linens and stuff."

"If that's what it is."

"Wait a minute. We'll see."

I brought back the ashtray full of keys. Some were obviously too old, long iron keys with curlicued heads and intricately notched ends. Three were too small to fit the lock. The rest, about a dozen, were assorted door and padlock keys. I tried them one by one. None worked.

"So much for that idea." Will stood. "It sounds like the rain's letting up again. Let's go phone."

"I want to see what's in here first. It might be something the police will want to know about."

"You have murder on your mind."

"Aren't you curious?"

"I am. But I also think we have enough explaining to do about breaking into the cottage, much less breaking into your cousin's private possessions. If it's locked and the key hidden, she mustn't want anyone to see what's in there."

"But that's just the point. What if *she's* in there?"

"Then the police are the ones who should open it."

"And if they come all the way down here to open it and it is just pillows or something? We'll look pretty stupid."

"Wait a minute. I think I saw a key somewhere else. Where it didn't belong." Will left the room. I heard him open a drawer in the kitchen and the clinking of cutlery as he pawed through it. A minute later he was back, brandishing a key in his hand.

"A Chubb. This might fit."

And it did. The lock sprang apart. I flipped open the catches at each end of the trunk but stopped before lifting it.

"Do you want to open it?"

Will pulled at his beard. "Let's do it together."

"All right. At the count of three."

We heaved at the lid. It stuck for a moment, then flung back. "A quilt." Will sighed.

"It's very old." I traced the pattern of stitches with one finger. This velvety patch might have been from a red dress my grandmother wore; this striped flannel may have been my great-grandfather's favourite shirt. I lifted it out with care. Underneath were some objects wrapped in newspaper.

"I wonder how old these papers are?" Will read the masthead. "It's last week's *Globe.*"

"What's inside?"

Will tore off the paper. Inside was an ugly piece of pottery, dull red in colour. It was part of a broken bowl. "Why would she want to save this?" He unwrapped another parcel. Another broken dish.

"What else is in there?"

I put down the quilt to help with the unpacking. A shoebox yielded a horde of pointed stones.

"Arrowheads." Will ran his thumb along the blades. "Still sharp."

Inside a blue Birk's box, nestled in white tissue, was an intact pot, about the size of a kettle. Around its fluted rim and continuing down the curve of its bowl was a series of black lines, etched in repeating patterns of short straight strokes which leaned one way and then the other.

"There's something inside." The mouth was wide enough for my hand to fit in easily. I pulled out a handful of corn kernels, blackened and dried.

"This is beautiful," Will said. He laid the pot reverently in its bed of tissue.

"What do you suppose is in here?" I shook an oblong Eaton's box. Inside, a heavy shape shifted.

"Be careful," Will warned. "It might break."

I peeled off the tape that held the lid closed and folded back several layers of green and red tissue. "Look at this," I breathed. Inside was a bead necklace, its centrepiece a shell the size of my hand. On its shimmering surface, a face had been etched, one eye closed in a monstrous leer.

I laid the shell back down in its nest of tissue and picked up a purple drawstring bag. It held more beads, some made of pottery and shell, some of a reddish metal I guessed was copper. A number of rings of the same metal were strung together on a length of knotted twine.

Will had picked out a shoe box. He posed with his thumbs on the lid before flipping it open. "Ta ra," he crowed, like a small boy on Christmas morning.

The box contained seven objects wrapped tightly in more coloured tissue paper. He unwrapped them one by one and laid them on the bed: six clay pipes whose bowls were decorated with striated lines much like the pot we'd uncovered first, and one carved out of dull green stone that had been scored with concentric bands.

"What's in this big package?" I peeled back several layers of newspapers to reveal a large object wrapped in a green garbage bag.

"Careful." Will helped me lift it out on the bed.

It wasn't particularly heavy but its contents rattled as they shifted. The garbage bag had been slit open and taped on one long side. Will used his pocket knife to slice the tape and I peeled back the plastic to reveal a common canvas sack, stencilled with the name and logo of a cereal company. It had been loosely sewn shut with the same twine used to hold the rings. I picked the stitches apart. Inside were yellow bones. Human bones.

NINE

"They're not hers," Will said.

"No kidding." I stared at the skeleton, the skull sitting on top of a haphazard collection of larger bones, limbs and ribs and pelvis jumbled together. The jaw gaped in a wide, nearly toothless smile. I shivered, and closed the bag.

"This stuff belongs in a museum." Will sat back on his heels. He picked up the bowl and turned it over and over in his hands. Red dust filtered down. "Or in a grave."

"Do you think this is the loot from that site she excavated? She could have brought the evidence up here to hide it."

"How? Smuggled it across the border? Why would she risk getting caught?"

"Where else could it be from?"

Will shrugged.

"We'd better put everything back before she gets here." I tried to lace the twine through the canvas but my fingers fumbled, trembling and useless.

"Why not confront her with it right away? Get everything out in the open."

"Because I want to give her a chance to explain herself." I used the back of my hand to push my hair out of my eyes. "I don't care if it's not smart, or what you think I should do. I've never had a family of my own. She's in trouble, granted, but that doesn't change the fact that she's my only cousin."

"There's Hank."

"He doesn't count. He's too young and the relationship's too vague. I just want to meet her and talk to her. There could be some other explanation for these things being here. She's only accused of looting artifacts; she hasn't been convicted yet."

"Yet," Will repeated.

"The least we can do is listen to her," I said. "Calmly and without prejudice."

"If that's the way you want to play it ... but we will have to tell the police about this."

"On Monday, okay? There's no phone to call from here anyway." I picked up the garbage bag, then dropped it. "I don't feel right about putting the bones back in this. It seems sacrilegious or something."

"Here," Hank pulled a red wool blanket out of the tangle of sheets. "Wrap it in this."

While I folded the wool gently around the canvas bag, Will began to roll the pipes in their tissue wrappings. "What if these relics are from around here? What if the surveyors stumbled over an ancient graveyard and she's been collecting ever since, planning to use them to finance her court case?"

"Then why would she be so anxious for me to sell the property?"

"Could be there's more wherever these came from."

"But she only came up north recently, she said. When would she have had time to dig them up? And the survey was done in the fall after she'd returned to the States."

"If she owned the property, she could dig at her leisure."

"There's a law about graveyards. What was it Bonnie said?"

"Why were you talking to her about graveyards?"

I sat back, thinking. "A couple of months ago she brought home some articles about aboriginal sites from the museum. I found them on the kitchen table. They were fascinating, although mostly about the States. She didn't want to talk about it, said she gets enough of that at work, but I was really interested. Appropriation of voice and all that. It's a big issue around the English Department these days."

He put the box of pipes back into the trunk. "So what does literature have to do with bones and pottery?"

"It's a question of what belongs to whom. Some people that Bonnie works with think that repatriation of museum collections is wrong, that too much history will be lost if relics go back to reserves where people maybe don't have the resources or skills to care for them properly. And others agree with native communities who feel that their heritage has been desecrated and stolen, and they want it back. And then there are collectors who don't care one way or the other but who'll pay big bucks for genuine artifacts."

"And what was Bonnie's opinion?"

"She said it was complicated because sometimes the sites were of people who've disappeared, been killed by war or disease so that there's no one left to claim a relationship to the find except the descendants of their enemies, native and white. That in that case, it should be finders' keepers."

"Sounds like a license to loot to me."

"She has a point," I defended my friend. "Someone has to look after the past. Anyway, I don't remember all the details, but I believe bones have to be left in place or properly reburied by the native descendants. Whatever, there's a lot of paperwork involving different government departments, as well as trying to figure out which native community has jurisdiction over the find."

"All that paperwork would tie up any development."

"And who would want to buy a cottage on the site of a graveyard?" I shivered. "Ghosts."

"Not exactly a place for R and R."

We contemplated the treasures spread out on the bed.

"I'd think a find like this would be pretty rare, these days," I said. "All these pieces are in perfect condition. They'd be worth a lot of money to a private collector."

"How old do you think they are?" Will picked up the big shell and traced the face with one finger.

"Could be hundreds of years," I said. I slipped my baby finger through one of the rings. It caught at the middle knuckle. "I don't know who all lived in this area, but it's been settled by whites since the mid-1800s."

"Well, let's put it all back until your cousin gets here and can explain where it comes from." Will rewrapped the necklace. I poured the rest of the jewellery into the drawstring bag.

Headlights flashed across the window.

"Oh no, it's her. How are we going to explain why we're looking through her trunk?"

"The truth," Will said. A car door slammed. "You go on out and greet her. I'll clean this up a bit. She's the one with questions to answer."

"But it's her house. We were sneaking into her things."

"It's your house," he corrected me. He pushed me lightly towards the door. "Go on, now. It will be better if you meet her first, before we have to get into all this."

A flurry of knocking rattled the building. I wondered why she didn't just walk in. I closed the bedroom door on Will, and took a couple of deep breaths. "Hello, Marilyn," I practiced in my mind. "Who's the skeleton in your closet?"

I was still smiling to myself when I opened the back door.

"Bonnie! What are you doing here?" My shout brought Will running.

Bonnie grinned at me, then bit her lip. In the short walk from the driveway to the house, the rain had plastered her hair to her head and soaked the white fisherman's knit sweater she wore so that it sagged from her shoulders almost to her knees.

"I'm glad to see you, too," she said.

"You'd better come in." I opened the door wider and stood back.

Bonnie ducked her head. She fiddled with a strand of hair, then flipped it behind her. She stared at me. "The kids are in the car. Can I bring them too?"

"What's going on, Bonnie?" Will loomed out of the shadows behind me.

From the dark driveway came a faint cry, "Mom? Mom? Where are you? Mom?"

"I'll explain everything. Just let me bring the kids in, okay? Megan's half-asleep and Ryan's terrified of the storm."

We couldn't very well turn them away, not at this late hour. The presence of the Hazlitt family would make it impossible for us to question Marilyn about the artifacts when she arrived. If she arrived.

"Have you eaten?" I asked.

"Yeah, thanks." She turned and ran through the rain back down the path.

"You'd better unroll the mattresses on the bunks," I said to Will. "Bonnie and the kids can share the bunk beds."

"What about us?"

I shivered. "I don't want to sleep in that room. We can camp out in the living room on the sofa bed."

The boy came running up the path, head ducked against the rain, a school bag bouncing on his back. He clutched a brown toy bear to his chest. He hid it behind his back as soon as he saw us. "It's my sister's," he muttered.

He stood just inside the door, looking down at his feet, his thin shoulders shivering inside the light black jacket he wore over a gray track suit. I knew he was nine, but he was small for his age and wiry, with thick, curly black hair, neatly cut. He must take after his father in looks as his sister took after her mother with her blonde chubbiness. Bonnie staggered under her weight up the path. Will ducked out to take the child, but she clung to her mother, her face burrowed in the collar of Bonnie's sweater.

"It's okay," Bonnie said to Will. "She's not that heavy."

"Come in by the fire," I gestured towards the front room. "You look like you're all freezing."

"Mom rented a car with a busted heater," the boy said. "No big surprise."

"Ryan," Bonnie groused, "I've had just about enough of you for today." She put Megan down inside the door and turned to us, smoothing her face into a social smile. "These are my kids, as you've guessed. Ryan and Megan. Say hello to Mr. and Ms. Cairns, Megan."

The little girl shook her head.

"I'll get the beds ready," Will said. He turned to Ryan. "Want to help?"

The boy glanced at his mother, then back to his feet. He didn't reply. Will waited for a moment, then turned away.

Bonnie sighed. "I've got to go back down to the car to get our sleeping bags," she announced. "Ryan, take your sister and go with Ms. Cairns. I'll only be a minute."

Megan began to cry, a hopeless sniffling. Bonnie peeled the child's hands from the grip around her waist, then knelt down beside her. "Everything will be all right," she murmured. "I just have to get our things from the car and then we can all go to bed. In the morning there'll be the lake and a beach and lots of things to explore. It'll be fun."

"I want to go home," Megan wailed. She began to cry even louder.

"Oh, hell," Ryan swore. He pushed past me and went to stand at the picture window, staring through his own reflection into the darkness.

"Ryan," Bonnie pleaded. "Your language."

He ignored her. She sighed again and bent back over her daughter, trying to soothe her cries.

I heard Will punching the mattresses flat on the bunk beds. It seemed to be taking a lot of effort.

"Give me your keys," I said to Bonnie. "I'll get your things from the car while you get the kids settled."

"It's all right. I'll do it."

"Don't be ridiculous. You stay with your children. It'll only take a minute."

"Thanks." She handed me a ring of two keys. "One's for the trunk. The doors aren't locked. We don't need everything; just the sleeping bags and the blue backpack. Oh, there's a box of groceries too on the back seat, milk and cereal, hot dogs ... I didn't know what you might have."

"There's lots of chili," Will said. "Plenty for everyone."

I looked out at the rain. It was coming down hard, and beyond the small circle of light by the door it was very dark. I stepped out on the stoop under the overhang of the porch. A cold wind blew in from the lake, rattling tree branches and flapping the tarpaulin on the car parked by ours in the drive. Beneath the odour of wet earth and composting leaves was another scent I couldn't identify but which reminded me of hamburger left too long at the back of the fridge.

Will joined me. "I'll help."

"You just want to get away from Bonnie and her lovely children."

"She's your friend," he retorted.

I sighed. "I know. Well, I'll go get a couple of those garbage bags from the kitchen. We can use them as rain capes."

Bonnie had the two kids with her on the rag rug in front of the fire. Ryan was busy stabbing the smouldering embers with the poker. Megan had stopped crying. She leaned heavily against her mother, her thumb in her mouth, her eyes wide on the dancing flames.

Will and I held the garbage bags over our heads and made a dash for the parking area. The path was slippery and my shoes were soon wet through. The three cars were parked in a straight line, the tented one in the middle between our Honda and a Ford so white it seemed fluorescent.

Will fumbled with the keys. When the trunk opened, a small interior light shone on a jumble of bulging suitcases and bags of books and toys.

"Looks like she's planning a long holiday," he said, his tone carefully neutral.

"I didn't know anything about this." I dropped my plastic cape and reached for the sleeping bags which were stuffed under the overhang of the back window.

"What do you think she's up to?"

I shrugged.

"And where's Robin?" Will continued.

"How should I know? I'm getting soaked. You get the groceries. I'll take these back to the house."

With the pack over one shoulder and my arms full of sleeping bags, I couldn't hold on to the plastic. I let it fall to the ground. My eyes had accustomed themselves to the dark and I could make out the line of the path back to the house with its welcome promise of warmth and light. By the time I reached the door, I was drenched. From the curses following me, I knew Will was too.

Bonnie met us at the door. "Thanks," she said again. "Megan's just about asleep. I'll get the kids settled and then we'll talk."

"You bet we'll talk." I dumped my load inside the second bedroom door. "You'll all have to fit in here."

"Fine." Bonnie knelt to unroll the bags and looked up at me through a curtain of hair. "I really appreciate this, Rosie. I can't tell you how much it means to me."

I just shook my head. I had a feeling I knew what my friend was up to and I didn't like it, not one bit.

Will was back in Marilyn's bedroom, peeling off his soaked shirt and pants. He had brought our suitcases in here along with a pile of towels he'd pulled from the wardrobe. The heat from the fire had done nothing to warm the damp chill of this room and I dried and dressed as quickly as I could. I kept my eyes away from the bed and its awful secrets.

"What'll we do about Marilyn?" Will whispered.

"She'll have to wait." I toweled my hair vigorously. "A few more minutes now can't hurt. And we've got to find out what Bonnie's doing here."

"An outhouse!" Ryan's voice rose in outrage. "You've got to be joking."

"Pretend you're camping," Bonnie snapped. "Take the flashlight and wash your hands in the kitchen when you come back in."

"You're not making her go out there."

"Megan's a baby," Bonnie began, but was interrupted by the little girl, "No, I'm not."

"Just go, Ryan. No more arguments."

The screen door slapped and feet splashed angrily through puddles. A thin wavery light passed the window of our room.

Will and I looked at each other. He put his hand on my shoulder and I suddenly threw my arms around him. We hugged hard.

"What a hassle," I whispered fiercely, "So much for our romantic night at the cottage. I'm sorry."

Will didn't answer, but his grip tightened. I felt his lips on my hair.

The screen door banged again.

"There's spiders out there," Ryan shouted. "And it stinks. It's gross."

"Did you use it?" his mother replied.

"Well, yeah," the boy mumbled. "I had to go the bathroom, didn't I?"

"Then just go to bed, okay? We'll talk in the morning."

"This is so dumb, this whole trip. They don't want us here. It's obvious."

"Shush. That's not true. Rosie's my friend. It's just so late, that's all."

"We should go back to Grammy's house."

"We'll talk in the morning," Bonnie repeated, her voice sharp "Now get into your pyjamas and no more nonsense."

"Dad lets me stay up late when we go to Lynne's cottage."

"Well, I say it's late and time for you to go to bed. Hop to it. Right now."

Will and I met Bonnie in the hall. She shut the door to the bunk bedroom. In one hand, she carried a covered cooking pot. She saw me looking at it, and blushed.

"I'll just take this outside," she gestured with the other hand towards the door. "I ... I couldn't persuade Megan to go to the outhouse so I thought it would be okay to use this old pot. It is okay, isn't it?"

It was a little late to ask permission to use it now. I nodded briefly and turned to the living room.

Will rummaged in the kitchen. "We should have brought some scotch. I need a drink."

"I've got a bottle in the car," Bonnie came back in. She set the pot inside the bedroom door, then closed it tight. "I'll go down and get it."

She wrapped herself in a garbage bag and ran out. When she got back, she was out of breath, but she brandished a bottle of Glenfiddich in her hand.

"Thank the Lord for small mercies." Will brought three tumblers and a plastic jar of water over to the coffee table. He sat down beside me on the sofa.

Bonnie settled on the rug before the fire. She put her glass down on the stone hearth and hugged herself fiercely, shaking her hair so that raindrops flew, sputtering on the embers. I noticed she'd cut her hair after all, so that it hung only to her shoulders; not only that, but as it dried, I could see that she'd tried to change its colour, her natural blonde appearing as highlights in the new brunette dye.

"What have you done to your hair?" I asked.

She brushed it back from her face, but didn't reply.

"It looks like you've brought an awful lot of things for one weekend, even a long one. Is there a kitchen sink in the trunk, too?" Will tried to joke. Neither Bonnie nor I smiled.

"We'll leave in the morning," she muttered. "I wasn't planning to stop, but it's a long way from Ottawa and driving in that storm was no fun. I didn't think you'd mind putting us up for just one night."

"It's not that we mind," I objected. "But you could have

warned us that you were thinking of bringing them."

"There's no phone," Bonnie pointed out. "Besides, I figured the less you know, the better it is for you."

"Oh, Bonnie." I was too angry — and worried — to play games with her. "Does Harold know you've brought the kids here?"

She picked up the poker and viciously stoked the coals, pushing them into a heap under a green log that hissed and smoked instead of burning.

"Well?" I goaded her.

"They're mine too," she replied.

"But it's kidnapping. You could go to jail."

"Only if I get caught."

Will interrupted, "Where's Robin?"

"I don't know." She poured another drink. "He's supposed to meet us ..."

"You're not going to tell us anything, are you?" I asked.

"It's better for you not to know," she repeated.

"I can't believe you're doing this." I shook my head.

"Bringing them here? I told you, I had to get them out of the storm. And I thought you were my friend."

"I am. That's why I'm so worried. Where were you headed?"

"It doesn't matter."

"It does so."

"If you had kids, you'd understand."

"You're kidnapping them," I said, straight out.

Bonnie flushed. "It's not kidnapping when they're your own kids. I'm their mother. I know what's best for them."

"What's best for them?" I repeated. "Being snatched away from everything that's familiar, their schools and friends, to live a life on the run? Where will you live? How will you live? You know Harold will have the police looking for you."

"I've come into some money we can live on for awhile. Then I'll get a job."

"Doing what? And what will the kids do while you're working?"

"They'll be in school."

"Not all the time."

"Other single mothers manage."

"When they haven't any choice."

Bonnie didn't answer me. She drained her drink too quickly and burst into a fit of coughing.

"It's not too late to go back," I suggested when she regained her breath.

"Harold phoned me yesterday to tell me I could have the kids this weekend," she said. "As if he was granting me a great privilege and I should be on my knees thanking him for it."

"Is this all about you and Harold? What about the kids? Do they know you're not going back?"

She shook her head. "I think Ryan suspects. He's being very stubborn and hard to get along with. As you might have noticed."

The log collapsed with a hiss of sparks on its bed of coals. Will got up to add another. It was a length of birch and when its bark ignited, it crackled with blue flames. We all watched them flare and settle.

Bonnie began to cry, silently, the tears streaking her cheeks. "I just can't stand it any more. I thought if I said I'd leave Robin, Harold would let me have the kids, but he won't. He says that I gave up all rights to them when I left the house. He's getting married again. He says they need a real mother. I'm their mother. It's me they need." Her voice rose.

Ryan rushed across the room and hugged her. He glared at us. "What did you do to her?"

"It's not us..." Will began.

Bonnie shushed him. "It's all right, Ryan." She sniffled, wiping her sleeve across her face, smearing tears. "Go back to bed."

"What's all this about Dad?" he demanded.

"Were you listening? Don't you know it's rude to eavesdrop?"

"For goodness' sake, Bonnie," I said. "It's his life too you're talking about."

"He's only a child."

"I'm not a child, I'm almost ten." Ryan stood tall in his Batman pyjamas, his hands on his hips. He stared down at his mother, a frown creasing his forehead. "This is more than a holiday, isn't it? Dad doesn't know where we are?" His lips trembled, but he pressed them tightly together.

"It's for the best." Bonnie grabbed his hand and tried to

draw him down to her. He refused to bend.

"We want to go home, Megan and I. Back to Ottawa."

"Don't you love me?" She shook his hand so hard that he swayed on his feet. "I'm your mother. Don't you want to be with your own mother?"

Someone banged on the back door. We froze, staring at each other. There wasn't time for Bonnie or Ryan to hide, nor, for that matter, any place to hide them. The boy's face blanched, and now he did fall to his knees beside his mother. She put her arm around him and squeezed him to her.

"I won't let them go," she hissed.

TEN

Will stood. "It's probably Marilyn. At last." He went down the hall to open the door.

"Hey there." It was Hank. "You figured out a way to get in."

He pushed past Will and strutted into the room. In his long green waterproof cape, hat with a wide brim turned up on one side, and knee-high black rubber boots, he looked like a buccaneer — and he knew it. He stopped when he caught sight of Bonnie.

Will's face appeared over his shoulder. He shrugged in answer to my look which plainly asked why he had let Hank in.

"What's she doing here?" Hank asked.

"This is my friend, Bonnie Hazlitt," I said. "And her son, Ryan. Bonnie, Ryan, this is my ... my cousin, Hank McDonnel."

Bonnie glared at Hank. She had her arm around Ryan, holding his face tight against her shoulder.

"You scared us," she said. "Banging on the door like that."

"Who did you think it was? Police?" He looked at the bottle and glasses. "I could do with a drink."

"What do you want?" I asked him. "And how did you get here? I didn't hear any car."

He grinned. "I come by boat. I've got a camp along the lake a bit and it's easier to get here by water than through the woods. I figured you might need this to get in." He held up a key. "Marilyn leaves one with us up at the store."

Bonnie stood suddenly, pulling Ryan to his feet with her. "You'll excuse us. It's been a long day. We're going to bed." She pushed the boy past the two men. "Good-night Rosie, Will." The door slammed behind them.

"Friendly, isn't she? Not!" Hank took off his hat. "What about that drink, eh?"

"You waited long enough to bring us the key," Will grumbled. "We would have been pretty wet and cold by now if we hadn't found a way in."

"And just what way was that?" Hank glanced towards the porch. "Marilyn said she left the place locked up."

"You talked to her?" I stood up.

"Not her. The friend she's with called."

"Where is she? Is she all right?"

"You don't need to worry about Marilyn. She can look after herself. She'll be here sometime tomorrow." He looked around the room. "Seems like you've made yourselves comfortable. Found everything?"

Will and I glanced at each other. Could he possibly be hinting that he knew what was under the bed?

Will said. "We're fine. In fact, we were about to turn in ourselves."

"Marilyn won't like you being in her room. In her bed. She's particular about her privacy."

"We wouldn't dream of it," I snapped. "We're going to sleep out here. If it's any business of yours."

"Is it your business?" Will asked. He stared hard at Hank until the boy turned away, his hand brushing across his mouth.

"It's just Marilyn," he muttered. "She's a private sort of person."

"Thanks for the advice," Will said.

Hank replaced his hat. "I can see I'm not welcome. So much for thanking the messenger."

"Are you going back on the lake in the dark?" I asked. "Aren't you nervous?"

"I can get around here blindfolded. It's in the blood."

"Thanks for bringing us the key. If Marilyn had left us a note, you wouldn't have had to come out on such a night."

"A little bad weather doesn't bother me." He gestured towards the sofa. "You're going to sleep on that?" When we nodded, he added, "Sweet dreams, then."

Will slammed the bolt home on the door behind him. "Good riddance," he said. "What are you up to?"

I was about to knock on the second bedroom door. "I haven't finished talking to Bonnie." I didn't bother keeping my voice low. I wanted her to hear what I had to say.

"Haven't we all had enough tonight?" Will slumped against the wall.

"She's using those poor kids just as much as Harold is, for her own needs, not theirs. Someone has to show her that before it's too late."

I heard rustling behind the door, but it didn't open. Will heard it too.

"Let's give it a rest," he yawned elaborately. "I'm beat and so's Bonnie, I'll bet. Things will look different in the morning. Calmer."

"That's a cop-out." I yawned too, in spite of myself.

Will put his arm around me. "In the morning, when everyone's had a good rest." He leaned closer and whispered in my ear. "She won't be taking those kids anywhere else tonight. And we should give her a chance to sober up."

I trailed him back into the living room. He was already shifting the coffee table and pushing the sofa back to make room to pull out the mattress. I unrolled the sleeping bags and zipped them together to make a double bag.

"Oh, no," he pointed to the mattress. It was studded with rows of neat circles where the springs strained the fabric. "I'll get the quilt from Marilyn's bed to cushion them a bit."

I stretched. My head felt fuzzy. I wasn't used to drinking hard liquor. Wine and beer are more my style. "I'm going out on the porch for a minute. I need some fresh air."

The rain had let up at last, but a small wind continued to wring water in a steady dribble onto the roof. A full moon appeared fitfully between clouds. A motor roared, then settled into a steady puffing as Hank's boat headed down river. Far off over the darkness that was the lake, a loon cried out, the breathless gasp at the end of a long dying fall. Its ghost voice was answered by another and then another. Will came out to listen.

"It's so quiet here," he said. "You can't even hear the highway."

"And no boats on the lake, now that Hank's gone. Your parents' lake is so noisy, might as well be on the 401."

"It would be a shame to spoil it with speedboats and jet skis."

"I hate those things. They sound like dentists' drills on the water."

Will put his arms around me. I leaned back against the solid trunk of his body, feeling safe. The loons stopped calling but the night was alive with skitterings under the trees, the whisper of leaves overhead.

"Let's go to bed," he whispered into my hair.

We stripped quickly and snuggled for warmth. I wrapped my legs around his. His mouth was on my breast. As our bodies shifted, turning into each other, the bed frame began to squeak. We stopped moving.

My eyes had adjusted to the dark. I could see Will's face below mine, his mouth quirked in a smile.

"It's kind of noisy," I whispered.

"You think they're asleep yet?"

"I don't know."

We kissed again. The bed began to thump the floor in rhythm. I began to laugh, trying to smother my giggles against Will's bare shoulder. After a moment, he laughed too.

I flopped down beside him. The bed protested.

"I'm sorry," I said. "I can't ... with this bed and them in the next room."

"It's like camp. Sneaking around."

"Goodnight then."

"Goodnight."

We rolled spoon fashion, his arms around me, his breath soon even against my neck. It took me much longer to fall asleep.

Something bumped against the cottage wall.

I was awake, straining to see through the dark.

Bump again. A dragging slide.

"Will." I poked him in the ribs. "Will. Wake up."

He moaned and rolled over.

"Will."

"What is it?"

"There's someone outside."

"What?" He was awake now, rubbing his eyes, yawning.

"Listen."

A moment later, it came again. A thump, a drag, a dry cough.

Will sat up and reached for his pants. I grabbed my glasses and shirt.

"He's around the back." Will said. "We can sneak out through the front door and corner him."

"You think it's Hank?"

"Could be. He might be trying to give us a scare."

"Why?"

"Who knows?" Even in the dark, I sensed Will's shrug. "This is turning out to be some night."

We tiptoed out to the porch and eased the screen door open. It was a long step down to the granite ledge. The rock was cold on my bare feet, and slippery with the rain.

Will squeezed my hand and pointed along the front of the cottage. "I'll wait here till you reach the far corner," he whispered. "If we both appear at the same time, we'll take him by surprise."

I ran past the picture windows, pausing at the corner to wave to Will. He waved back, then slipped into the shadows of the porch.

I took a deep breath and scooted around to the back door.

At first I thought it was a bear standing there on all fours, rubbing itself against the wall beneath Marilyn's bedroom window.

"Bossie," Will shouted. "Get out of there. Coo-ee."

He slapped a stick against a rock. That startled the cow. She lifted her head and lowed.

Another answered right behind me. I jumped, turning in mid-air. Close up, these cows were huge. And they had horns.

"What'll we do?" I shouted to Will.

"Chase 'em."

He walked right up and whacked the cow nearest him on the rear. She leaped, her tail slashing. For a moment, I thought she would run him down, but she turned away towards the drive.

"Don't let them go round the front. We've got to herd them down the road through the gate." Will slapped the cow again. She broke into a trot, tossing her head and moaning.

I waved my arms and jumped up and down. The animal in front of me shook its head from side to side. I wondered if it was a bull. I also wondered where I could run to if it decided to chase me.

It raised its tail and pissed. The stink rose in the darkness.

"Get," I screamed at it. "Move."

"What's happening?" Bonnie opened the back door.

"Cows," I told her. "Didn't you close the gate at the end of the driveway?"

"Is that what it was for?"

The cows decided that three humans were too many. They lumbered down the hill towards the car. Will followed, whipping his switch and calling over and over, "Hoo, Bossie. Go, Bossie." His bare torso gleamed white in the moonlight. "Get the flashlight, Rosie," he called back over his shoulder. "And my shirt. It's freezing out here."

I brushed past Bonnie on my way to the livingroom.

She grabbed my arm to stop me. "Rosie."

"What now? Can't you see we're busy?"

"I'm sorry. I shouldn't have brought the kids here."

"It's a little late for that. Will was right: we'll talk in the morning."

"I just didn't know what else to do. We had to pass this way; it was so late, the kids kept arguing..." Her voice rose.

"It's okay, Bonnie." I could hear Will herding the cows down the drive. The flashlight was on the kitchen table. I pulled free of her grasp and scooped it up, along with Will's shirt which he'd dropped on the floor on his side of the sofa.

"You might as well go back to bed," I added. "It may take a while to get all the cows back on the other side of the fence."

Even as I spoke, a cow galloped past the picture window out front, Will stumbling along behind it. "Rosie," he yelled. "Where are you?"

"Coming," I called. "Get some rest," I suggested. Bonnie grabbed my arm.

"It's just..." she began. "Well, it's that boy who was here. Who was he?"

"Hank? He's a cousin twice removed, or something. Why?"

"I thought I recognized him." No longer talking about her

own problems, her voice grew stronger.

"I can't imagine where ... did you stop at that corner store on the way up? He works there, for his grandfather."

"No, we came straight here."

"How did you know where to find us? We almost missed the turn, even with the map."

"I told you I'd been up to this lake before. I remembered Roger showing us the road to this place. It's got quite a local reputation, you know."

"I didn't know."

She waved her hand airily. "Everyone used to talk about the haunted house and family feud between the McDonnels and Bakers. And people used to come down the lake to get Mrs. Baker to tell their fortunes. She was quite a character."

"You met her? Why didn't you tell me?"

"It was just the one time. I'd forgotten about it until you showed me the map. But what I wanted to tell you was that I'm sure I've seen that boy before, at the museum."

"Hank? He doesn't seem the type to be interested in dinosaurs."

"Oh, he wasn't a tourist. And he wasn't in the galleries. He had an appointment with one of the archaeologists."

"Are you sure?"

"I couldn't mistake that hair."

"He must have been going to see someone, maybe about the relics ..."

"What relics?" Her eyes brightened, curious.

"Rosie," Will called. He sounded very angry.

"Tell me." She grabbed my arm.

I shook her off. "Later. When Marilyn gets here. It's her business. I've got to go help Will."

"Do you mean Indian relics? Pottery? Bones?"

"Yeah, that sort of stuff. Look, later, okay?"

"Where are they?"

"Rosie, will you please come and help?" Will was at the back door, switch in his hand, mud spattering his good pants.

"I've got to go." I pushed her, none too gently, in the direction of the bedroom. "We'll talk in the morning."

She opened her mouth to add something, but changed her mind and returned to her bed.

"How're your feet?" I asked Will.

"Wet." He handed me a second switch. "I think the cows are ready to leave. Just keep the switch moving and keep your voice low and even. I don't think they'll go into the trees unless they get scared."

"When did you learn so much about cows?"

"Misspent youth." We'd reached the drive where the cows were milling about the cars. There were six of them, one a calf. "Hoo-ee," Will carolled. He snapped the switch. The cows shuffled and lowed, but moved off down the hill toward the gate. "Remember my friend Arnie? His Dad had a dairy farm. I used to help out sometimes."

The cows lumbered along, the two of us following, whistling our switches when they slowed or threatened to leave the path. I gave up trying to avoid the puddles.

Now that the rain had stopped, the night was still and cool, silent except for the plodding and complaining herd. Once they were through the gate, I pulled it shut and looped the chain over the post so that it wouldn't open again.

Will shivered. "It's cold."

"Yeah."

We held hands walking back up the drive but had to pass single file between the parked cars. Between the white Ford and our Honda, Marilyn's car squatted like a turtle beneath the green shell of the tarp.

"What kind of car do you think this is?" Will ran his hand along the low rooftop and down over the tiny trunk.

"Probably a Miata. I've always wanted one of those. Bright red."

"Some kind of sports car, for sure." He felt the door handle under the cloth. "It's locked."

"What did you expect? She wouldn't go to the bother of covering it up and then not lock it."

"Seems a bit paranoid to lock up way out here. No one's going to come down that road."

"We did. And so did Bonnie."

"Yeah, Bonnie. Some friend you have. You realize you could be arrested for assisting her in kidnapping those kids."

"It's not really kidnapping. They are hers."

"But her husband has custody."

"I thought you said we'd had enough talking tonight."

"Okay." He slapped his shoulder. "Bugs are still bad. I hoped they might quiet down after dark."

"Only mosquitoes do that. Black flies feast by moonlight." I spread my arms and vamped, "I vant to bite your neck."

"Not a bad idea. Ouch," He smacked his ear. "That one really hurt. Time to go in."

"Bonnie told me something funny just now when I was getting the light," I said, as we trudged up the path to the back door.

"Oh?" He paused to let me catch up.

"She saw Hank at the museum."

"Hank? Is she sure?"

"She thinks he had an appointment with one of the staff archaeologists."

"Must have been about those relics."

"That's what I said. But if he wanted to give them to the museum, why are they still under Marilyn's bed? And how did he find out about them in the first place?"

"He has a key to the cottage. Maybe he found them and didn't know what they were."

"Do you think she knows he knows about them?"

"Beats me." Will held the screen door open for me.

"Give me the flashlight. I have to use the john."

A stray gust shook down a shower from the leaves. I stood for a moment looking through the gap between the trees at the still blackness that was the water. Nothing moved. Out on the lake, the loons began to laugh.

ELEVEN

I never sleep well in a strange bed. This night proved no exception. I tossed and turned, unable to stop thinking about the relics in the trunk, Bonnie's desperate flight, and my cousin's mysterious absence. I finally drifted into a kind of sleep before dawn. The clamor of birds rising from the marsh jolted me awake. My jaws ached. I'd been dreaming again of chewing toffee and, as I chewed, my teeth one by one loosened and fell out. I was so convinced by the reality of the pain that I ran a finger over all my teeth right away. All were there; none were loose.

Will still slept, curled away from me in a protective ball. I heard footsteps in the hall, the muffled squeak of the back door opening: Bonnie or Ryan going to the outhouse. Gray light filled the room. A crow cleared its voice over and over. I snuggled down in the sleeping bag, waiting for whoever had gone out to come back. I dozed off.

When I woke for the second time, it was much brighter, the sky a clear pale blue, blushing pink at its horizon, and decorated with wisps of cloud. I dressed quickly and went out to the outhouse myself. Birdsong racketed. I recognized the most common — the robins, redwinged blackbirds, jays, gulls, and loons — but they accounted for only a fraction of the chorus that greeted the rising sun.

As quietly as I could, I made a pot of coffee and took my

cup out to the screened porch. It was furnished simply with a wicker table and two matching rockers, which were surprisingly comfortable. I sat and sipped, looking out over the marsh at the glint of sunlight on the lake water. Swallows swooped and spun over the rice beds. A great blue heron flapped lazily by, its knobby legs trailing. Down by the river, a blackbird trilled over and over, asserting his right to territory. Things were so peaceful I could almost imagine that the events of last night were part of some nightmare.

"Hi," a small voice piped up. "Can I come out here with you?"

I turned to see Megan standing by the porch door. She was still in pyjamas. Her teddy bear dangled from one hand, a faded pink baby blanket from the other.

"Sure. Want some breakfast?"

She shook her head. I watched how precisely she closed the door behind her and walked over to the window where she stood with her nose against the screen. I wondered if she might be short sighted. I got my first pair of glasses when I was seven; I could still remember my amazement when the blur of colour that surrounded me resolved into leaves and letters and people's faces.

"Is your Mom up yet? Or Ryan?"

She shook her head.

I sipped my drink. I wasn't used to talking to children. "Does your bear have a name?"

"It's not real, you know," she informed me. "It's only a toy."

"But a special toy."

She treated that remark with the disdain it deserved. But she did hitch the bear up so that it, too, could look out the window.

"His name's T. Bear," she informed the outside. "Where's the beach? Mommy said we could make sand castles."

"You can't see it from here. We have to take the boat down the river to its end."

"Do you have a boat?"

"There's a canoe on the dock."

"Are you an Indian?"

"No. Why?"

"Indians paddle canoes. Made out of tree bark."

"That's right, in the olden days. The canoe here is made out of aluminum. Metal."

"It'll sink. Metal's heavy."

"Not that heavy."

"Oh." She wandered around the room looking alternately out the window and down at the pattern of dust whorls that lay thick on the board floor. She reached the second rocker and, after a moment's hesitation, climbed into it. With one foot, she set it rocking. She wrapped the bear in the blanket and held it closely, her thumb in her mouth.

"There you are," Bonnie said. She came in the room, a smile struggling to displace the panic on her face. "I couldn't imagine where you went."

I noticed that the cuffs of her pink sweat pants were wet and stained with grass.

"Been out for a walk?" I asked.

She looked down, rubbing one ankle down the other calf. "Just to the river and back. The grass is still pretty wet."

"We're having a conversation," Megan announced.

Bonnie glanced at me. "That's nice. Would you like your breakfast out here?"

"Okay."

Bonnie turned to me as she was about to leave the room. "Listen, Rosie, I'm sorry about last night."

I wondered if she meant their unexpected and unwelcome arrival or the business with the cows. "It's all right."

She nodded and went in. Megan and I rocked silently.

She asked suddenly, "Don't you have children?"

"No."

"Why not?"

"Some people do and some don't." I shrugged. "It's the way it is."

"I'm going to have six children. All girls."

"You'll be very busy."

"It'll be all right. They'll have two Mommies. Just like me."

I looked at her. She was rewrapping the bear with great concentration, tucking in the ends of blanket so it wouldn't trail.

"You've got two mothers?" I repeated.

"Oh yes, I've got Mommy and Lynne. She lives with us.

Ryan says we can't talk about her."

"Why not?"

"Mommy gets upset. I don't know why. Lynne's nice. She makes Daddy laugh."

Bonnie backed into the room, both hands occupied with large bowls of steaming oatmeal. Ryan followed her.

"You can have my chair," I told him. "I've got to wake Will."

"He's already up and out," Bonnie said.

"We need to talk," I said to her.

"In a bit. Let's eat in peace, okay?"

I left the three of them to their cereal and went back indoors. Will was re-assembling the sofa.

"How'd you sleep?" I asked.

He glanced up, his mouth twisted in a grimace. "Not the most comfortable night I've ever had. How about you?"

"I had my tooth falling out dream last night."

"That's what kept jabbing me in all my tender places: loose teeth."

I threw a pillow at him. "Don't be an idiot."

He tucked the pillow into the sofa corner and straightened, one hand on the small of his back. "You've made coffee already?"

"Want some?"

"You bet."

He rolled up the sleeping bags and carried them with our back packs into Marilyn's room. "They'll be out of the way in here," he explained.

"What are we going to do?" I handed him a cup. He didn't sit, but stood, drinking coffee and staring out the kitchen window at the woods.

"About what? Bonnie? Marilyn? The bones under the bed?"

"I assume Marilyn will have some explanation for them," I answered. "When she gets here."

"If she gets here," Will replied gloomily.

"You don't think she'll show up?"

"Hard to say. She seems to have a talent for avoiding you."

"Hank said she'd be here today."

"Speaking of which," Will turned away from the window, "I don't like the idea of leaving you here alone. Whatever Bonnie decides to do. Your cousins...both of them..."

"I can handle them." I said, beginning to get angry.

"I've got no doubt about that," Will laughed. "I'd hate to see any of them try to get around you when you get going." He put his coffee cup down and rubbed his beard. "I have to admit, though, I'm curious. And I don't want to go to my parents' place anyway."

"But they're waiting for you."

"I'll go see them and explain. It would be easier if they had a phone, but I shouldn't be more than three hours or so. I'll come back after lunch. Maybe Bonnie will have worked out by then what she's going to do and your cousin will have turned up. And we can get this whole mess sorted out."

"My hero," I chirped.

"Idiot," he kissed me.

"Excuse me," Ryan drawled, backing out of the kitchen.

Will and I broke apart. How did parents manage to find time for intimacy with kids around? I realized that childlessness was not without its advantages after all.

"Did you want something?" Will asked the boy.

"Can we go down to the beach?"

"In a while," I replied. "I have to talk to your mother."

"How come there isn't a TV here? Or even a radio? It's dead boring." He scuffed his shoes.

"There's a lot of books and magazines on that bookshelf in your room. As well as some games and puzzles, I think."

"Baby stuff."

"Why don't you explore the woods, then?"

The boy sighed. Bonnie came in and tried to hug him. He ducked away from her arms.

"We've got Nintendo at home," he said. "And Frank was going to come over today to play my new Mario game. He knows how to beat the fourth level."

"You spend too much time playing those games. The whole outdoors is here." Bonnie flung her arms wide.

"There's too many mosquitoes. And there's nothing to do. It's boring. I hate it. I wish we never came." He stomped back into the bedroom.

"Don't say a word," Bonnie warned us. She took a deep breath and marched down the hall. "Ryan," we heard her say and then the door closed on their talk.

"I'd better get going," Will said.

"Do you think you should stop at the store and call Robin? Or Harold?"

"I think we'd do well to keep out of this mess as much as possible."

Bonnie returned, Ryan behind her. She spoke in a carefully cheerful voice. "Ryan's going to take Megan down to the river to look for fish. And turtles. We brought our life jackets with us so they can go on the dock. Won't that be fun, honey?"

The little girl stood in the porch door, her thumb in her mouth. She looked from her brother to her mother and back before slowly nodding.

"Come and get dressed," Bonnie continued, "while Ryan goes to get the jackets."

"I'm not wearing one," he protested. "I know how to swim."

"So do I," said Megan.

"You'll both wear the jackets," Bonnie barked. "No argument."

Behind her back, Ryan rolled his eyes. Megan's lips trembled.

"I'll go with you down to the cars," Will put in hastily. "I have to leave for awhile and the sooner I go, the sooner I'll be back."

"Where are you going?" Bonnie asked.

"To see my parents. Their cottage is about an hour's drive north of here and they're expecting me today. I'm just going to visit with them awhile. I'll see you later."

"If you tell anyone we're here..." Bonnie looked more pathetic than threatening.

"It's your business, Bonnie. I think you're making a big mistake, but you know what's best for your kids."

"Like going home," Ryan interjected.

Bonnie ignored him. "Thanks, Will. Now come on, Megan, let's get some clothes on you."

"You'll be all right?" Will said softly to me.

"Sure, no problem. Drive carefully, will you?"

"I'll see you this afternoon."

We hugged and kissed. Ryan sighed loudly.

After they left, I puttered around the kitchen, making more coffee and considering the food we had on hand. There was enough chili for supper, if the friend Marilyn was apparently with didn't stay.

Bonnie shooed Megan out the door. Her shoulders slumped as if, with the kids gone, she could relax and let herself go.

"Coffee?" I asked her.

She took the cup I handed her and sank down in a chair at the table. I sat opposite. We both sipped and stared out the window at the play of light through the leaves. Far out on the lake, a motor boat cut a swath through the water. The hum of its engine rose and fell, scarcely louder than the buzz of mosquitoes which hovered in a cloud outside the screen porch.

"You agree with Will that I'm making a dreadful mistake, don't you?" Bonnie finally broke the silence.

I shrugged. What was the use of talking? I didn't think she would listen to what I had to say and I didn't want to lose my temper and alienate her. Mostly, I didn't want her to run away. Not just yet. Not until she'd had a chance to think things through.

"Robin thinks I'm wrong too," Bonnie continued. "He's had to apprehend kids and return them to the custodial parent. It's not pleasant."

I couldn't help myself. "Why didn't you think about that before you took off?"

"I did." She turned the cup around and around in her hand, staring into it as if reading a fortune in the dregs of black liquid. "All I've done is think about it. This is not a spur of the moment decision, no matter what you may think. I've been planning it for awhile, ever since ... well, I found out I could make enough money to get away. Robin agreed to help. I thought if we could go somewhere, not have to work for awhile, not have to worry about money, we could be happy again. Like we were in the beginning."

"With the kids?" I asked. "You're suggesting some kind of second honeymoon, and I can't see how Ryan and Megan fit into that."

"We weren't going to take them at first," Bonnie admitted. "You see how difficult Ryan can be. I thought Harold deserved him. But then, when Harold told me he was going to re-marry ..."

"That seems to me the solution to all your problems," I

objected. "Harold will have someone to help him look after the kids; they'll have a more stable home environment; and you'll be free to work out your problems with Robin."

"Leaving my children to some other woman? What kind of person do you suppose would want to marry my ex-husband? Just because she runs her own business, doesn't mean he can't walk all over her. I've told you what a control freak he is."

"What kind of business?"

She waved her hand in the air. "I don't know. Consulting or accounting or something like that."

"So maybe he's changed since you left and he's had to take care of the kids by himself. People do change. And this Lynne must be a pretty strong person in her own right if she can keep a business going in these times."

"She's probably desperate to get married. I mean, anyone who's thirty-five and still single has to be worried about missing the boat. And he's quite a catch, you know, owning his house and a steady job, early retirement coming up. He's in good shape for a man his age."

"Bonnie! I can't believe you're saying such things. You can't seriously believe all that. How do you know what she's like or what her life has been like? Have you even met her?"

She shook her head no.

"Then you can't know how she is with Harold or the kids. They seem to like her. Did Harold say anything about wanting to restrict visiting rights even more after he's married?"

"No. In fact..." Bonnie put her head in her hands, her hair curtaining her face.

"Well?" I prompted her.

She mumbled into her hands so that I had to strain to hear her. "He suggested that the kids might come to live with me while he's on his honeymoon. And that we might divide the summer holidays so that I have them for a whole month in the city."

"But isn't that just what you wanted? What does he say about Robin?"

"He said that finding himself in love with Lynne changed everything. He could see why I did what I did."

"You see? He's willing to bend a little, at last. You can have Robin and the kids and a career: everything. I don't understand why you have to run away. It'll just make Harold angry with you again, so that he'll become even more inflexible than he's been before."

"It's like all the rest of the things he's said don't count. The things he said in court about me being unfit. Now that he wants time to himself, it's all different. He acts like I should be grateful to him. Grateful that I'm going to be able to see my own kids more than once a month."

I sighed. "So who cares what his motives are? What counts is that you'll be with them more often. And that they get along with Harold's new wife."

"That's all Megan talks about. It's *Lynne says this* and *Lynne does that.* It's driving me crazy."

"Isn't it better than if this Lynne resented her new husband's children?"

"If she did, maybe he'd give them back to me."

"But half the time you say you don't want them."

"That's not true," she said. "You don't understand. Kids can drive you crazy, but when you're a mother, you forgive them, you can't live without them. I can give them just as good a home as Harold can. Better, even."

I shook my head. "I just don't see how you're going to live. Where is this money coming from?"

"Never mind that," she said. "That's my business." She clutched the dish towel to her face, as if to hide tears. "But what am I going to do now? Ryan's barely speaking to me. He hates me."

"He's frightened. He wants to go home. Why don't you take them back after the weekend? From what you say, Harold's willing to loosen up a bit..."

She drew back. "I'm not giving my kids up."

"I'm not suggesting that. If you take them away and get caught, you'll lose it all: the kids, your freedom, respect. This way, it's as if you just kept them for the weekend as Harold asked. Since you'll be seeing more of them, Ryan will stop resenting you and Megan will see you as a friend. Maybe you and Robin could move back to Ottawa and work out some sort of joint custody..."

"You don't know Harold. He'd never agree to that."

"He's already suggesting a more open arrangement," I

pointed out. I circled the table and knelt beside her chair, my arm around her. "Ryan's and Megan's needs have to come first," I insisted. "You and Robin have your own troubles to sort out. Do you think that will be easy with the kids along?"

She turned and clung to me. "I'm sorry. I didn't mean to lay all this on you."

"What else are friends for?" I hugged her. And why else did you come here, I wanted to ask, but didn't. "All you have to do is take them back to Ottawa and talk the situation over with Harold. I'm sure he'll listen to reason..."

"That's easy for you to say," Bonnie retorted. "What am I supposed to do? Call Harold and say, *Sorry, I took the kids, but I'll bring them home tomorrow?* You think he'll let it go at that? You think he won't punish me by not ever letting me have them again?"

"He's not totally unreasonable," I pleaded. "If you explain ..."

"You're so naive, Rosie," she said. "You have no idea what he's like."

"What who's like?" Ryan came in. He stopped short when he saw the tears on his mother's face. "Never mind." He turned to leave.

"It's all right," Bonnie straightened up, pushing her hair back behind her ears. "What do you want?"

"We want to go to the beach," Ryan mumbled. He wouldn't look at either of us.

The roar of a boat motor grew suddenly much louder, then faded before beginning again. We all looked out the window but could see nothing. A fisherman must have trolled in too close to shore and caught his propeller on the weeds.

"How about," I suggested, "I take Ryan and Megan to the beach in the canoe and you go up to the store to phone."

"Who are you calling?" Ryan demanded. "Dad? Or Robin?"

"I don't know," Bonnie replied.

"So when are we going home to Ottawa?"

"Do you really want to go back..." Bonnie's voice trailed off. "What about the trip we planned? You know I promised we'd go to Disneyland."

"That's for babies." Ryan fidgeted. "I don't want to drive all that way in that dump of a car. With Megan throwing up every time we hit a bump."

"That's not fair, Ryan. Megan's getting over being car sick."

"That's what you say 'cause you don't have to sit in back with her."

Bonnie sighed. "I'll think about it, okay?"

"And there's school," the boy continued. "I don't think Dad would be happy about me missing so much school if we leave now. There's over a month before summer holidays. I'll fail."

"Since when did you care so much about missing school?" She stood up, glancing out the door as she did so. "Where's Megan, by the way? She's not by the water by herself, is she?" Her voice sharpened.

"She said she'd stay on the dock."

"Oh, God." Bonnie jumped up.

Ryan and I followed her at a run down the hill to the river. Megan was nowhere in sight.

TWELVE

"Megan!" Bonnie screamed. "Megan!"

She leaned far over the edge of the dock, searching the water for a sign of the orange life jacket. Nothing. Upstream we could see a glint of white water: the rapids whose rushing murmur underscored the chattering birds and rustle of wind through reeds. The water — or someone diligent with a shovel — had carved a wide pool in front of the dock, deep enough for a swimming hole. The river narrowed again as it rounded a bend towards the open water, invisible to us behind a barrier of willows and wild rice.

"Megan! Megan!" We all shouted, then held our breaths, willing her to call. Only the shrieks of the gulls, angry at being disturbed, answered us.

Bonnie tried to forge her way along the riverbank, pushing the reeds aside and ignoring the wet mud that sopped up to her ankles. Ryan went the other way, upriver against the current, battling his way through the tangle of alders that crowded the shore. I ran back up to the cottage to check the outhouse. It was empty. I opened the shed. No one was inside, but there was a canoe paddle leaning against one wall and an old cork life float hanging from a hook above it. The paddle was a bit long for my taste and had a wide flat blade; the white jacket was water stained and missing one of its ties. I took it anyway. I hadn't been in a canoe for years, but hoped it was a skill like riding a bicycle.

I ran back to the river, praying that the canoe wasn't padlocked to a chain. For once luck was with me: it had been left untied, a long rope merely looped through an iron ring on the dock. Evidently, my cousin didn't fear unwelcome visitors on the river. I tipped the canoe over the edge of the dock into the water. It landed with a splash that got Bonnie's attention. She stopped fighting the muck and stood looking down river.

"Megan," she cried. "Baby, where are you?"

Ryan came back to the dock. "I can't get through the bush. I don't think she'd be able to either."

I put the paddle and float into the boat and sat down to take off my shoes. "She couldn't have gone very far on her own," I said. "She's got the life jacket on, doesn't she, Ryan?"

He nodded, swallowing hard to keep back the sobs that threatened him.

"Then, if she fell in, the current's carrying her out to the lake. I'll go look for her. If she's on land, she's probably not far away. Bonnie, why don't you drive up to the highway and call the cops. Maybe they've got dogs that can track her, if she's gone in the woods. Ryan, you wait at the cottage in case she gets back on her own."

Bonnie slogged back to firmer ground. She caught hold of her son as he turned towards the cottage.

"You stay in the house, you hear?" She shook him for emphasis. "Don't go looking around outside. I couldn't bear it if you got lost too."

"I'm sorry, Mom," Ryan began to cry in earnest. "I'm really sorry. I told her to stay right here. She promised." His voice rose in a wail of desperation.

"We're wasting time," I said. The canoe rocked as I lowered myself into it. I settled myself in the mid-section, kneeling on the metal ribs, the small of my back propped against a narrow cross bar.

Bonnie hugged Ryan fiercely and kissed the top of his head. "It'll be okay, boyo. She's probably back at the cottage now, wondering where we are."

"You call me if you find her," I shouted. I pushed off from the shore.

For a few seconds, I thought I'd be going nowhere. The canoe drifted broadside as I struggled to bring its bow around.

I'd never paddled such a big boat and never by myself. I'd seen it done, though. I paddled on each side to get the canoe headed in the right direction, then experimented with deep strokes followed by a slight trailing of the wide blade in the water. The bow dove into the weeds on the far shore. Cursing, I dug the paddle into the bottom and used it as a pole to push the boat back into deeper water.

"Rosie," Bonnie called.

Had she found Megan? I stopped paddling. The bow drifted around again. I struggled to keep from colliding with the overhanging branches of a willow tree, then gave up and grabbed one of them to hold the boat still.

Bonnie appeared on the dock. Her face had a strange still coldness that the tracks of tears did nothing to soften or hide.

"I can't get my car started," she said. "It turns over, but doesn't catch."

Ryan trailed her down the hill. "I told you we should have stopped for gas," he said.

"Even when the gauge reads empty, there's usually a few litres left in the tank as a safety measure," Bonnie defended herself. "At least, that's what your father always says. I thought we'd have enough ... "

"We're wasting time," I shifted to get the weight off my knees. They were sore from my fall through the window. That had happened only last night. It seemed ages ago.

"Do you have keys to your cousin's car? I could take it."

"I didn't see any around. She must have taken them with her. You'll have to walk up the road. It's only a mile or so. And maybe you'll find Megan on the way. It would make sense for her to follow the road if she's decided she wants to go home."

"It'll take forever to walk out to the store," Bonnie groaned.

"Then you'd better get going," I snapped. "The sooner you call the police and get some help down here looking for her, the sooner we'll find her. And don't forget to close the gate."

Bonnie stumbled back up the trail. I pushed off from the willow, rounded the bend, and headed for the open water, riding the river current and using the paddle on either side of the boat at times to keep it pointed in the right direction. By the time I passed the long stretches of reeds that marked the river mouth, I'd settled into a rhythm of stroke and drag that seemed to work; at least, I was going forward quickly.

The canoe scraped bottom and shuddered to a halt. I'd noticed a line of white plastic bleach bottles curving out into the lake, but hadn't realized their purpose: obviously, they marked a deeper channel through the sand bar I was now stuck on.

If I hit bottom then surely Megan, floating like an infant Ophelia on the current, would have struck ground here also. I clambered out of the canoe, wincing at the coldness of the water on my bare feet. It was barely ankle deep, the white sand packed into rills firm and barely yielding to my weight.

Hand to eyes, I surveyed the reed beds on either side. No colour but the green and. brown and blue of bullrushes and wild rice and water. I looked farther along the shores. To my left, the lake extended in a long curve, the marsh cutting deep into the woods which met it with a wall of dark pine and rock extending as far as I could see. There were cottages in that direction, I knew, but none could be seen from the river mouth.

To the right, a narrow finger of land, bordered by reed beds, stretched between river and beach. It seemed about a mile away across open water. And there, close to the strip of sand and bobbing on the waves was a boat.

"Of course," I said out loud. "Hank! It was his boat we heard a while ago. Megan must have begged him to take her to the beach. Why wouldn't he tell us he was taking her? You'd think he'd realize how scared we all are."

I glanced behind me, wondering if I should go tell Bonnie first that Megan was probably at the beach. The "probably" stopped me. I was too far away to see anyone on the shore; best make sure she was there and safe before following Bonnie up the road.

I dragged the canoe off the sandbar, ignoring the soaking my jeans got as I waded deeper into the water. Patches of weeds appeared, a soft slimy green that made me grimace when I stepped into them. I grasped the gunwales and heaved myself in. The canoe rocked dangerously, then righted itself. I dug in the paddle and headed straight for the patch of sand.

The windshield of the boat blinked as it rocked broadside on the waves. Funny that Hank wouldn't have pulled it up on the sand or anchored it out a bit deeper, I thought. Its keel must be getting a bit of a battering, not to speak of the propeller.

The wind had freshened and I bent my head as I worked, concentrating on the task of lifting and digging in the paddle, shifting my weight for balance as the canoe rose and fell on the waves. Long swells that broke in a froth of white, they rolled straight into the shore, pushing me in.

Every time I lifted the paddle, a bolt of pain shot through my left shoulder blade and slid down my spine. The wind chilled, while at the same time the sun bore into my back. I should have worn sunglasses. I should have changed into shorts. Wet denim clung to my calves. Water sloshed in the bottom of the canoe, some from waves that had splashed overboard, the rest from a leak I didn't want to think about. If I could only make it close enough to the beach to wade or even swim in, we could all go back in Hank's boat. He had said something last night about a camp along the shore. Perhaps that was where they were, back in the bush. Oh, I would give that young man a talking to he would never forget!

The canoe scraped bottom, then rocked as a particularly large whitecap caught it under the stern. I scrambled out, clutching the paddle in one hand and the rope in the other. The water was knee deep, the bottom soft sand dotted with broken clam shells, small rocks, and driftwood. I hauled the canoe right up out of the waves and wound the rope around the dead white branch of a stranded tree trunk.

I had landed about twenty yards from the other boat. Its motor was still down in the water, jarring each time the propeller struck bottom with the lift and fall of waves. Gulls circled overhead, quarrelling with each other, floating down towards the boat as if expecting to get a meal of fish. Once I went fishing with my friend Annie and her father up at Lake Simcoe. We didn't catch much but rock bass, perch and sunfish. I remembered the squall of white wings and hooked yellow beaks as her father broke the backs of the little fish and threw them overboard into the water. "Garbage fish for garbage birds," he said. Neither Annie's pleading nor my tears would make him stop. We finally refused to fish any longer and spent the rest of the day huddled in the bow of the boat, telling stories. Her father never took us fishing again.

The birds screamed. I ran to the speedboat, dodging logs white with guano and gray-green mounds of wild goose droppings. The beach itself was a narrow strip of exposed sandbar between the lake and a swamp whose black water rippled as the breeze blew over it. Beyond the swamp was woods, thick cedar woods here, a dark unbroken line of trees that leaned low over the reeds. Frogs hummed in chorus with the whine of stinging bugs, the complaints of gulls, the rhythmic slap of waves against the boat. I hesitated. Should I go to look for Hank's camp, or check out the boat? I was assuming it belonged to him and that he had Megan with him. I could be wrong on both counts. I would have to look in the boat.

It was grounded on the sand a few yards out from shore. A rope dangled at the bow. I gasped at the cold, hopping from one foot to the other through the shallows until I reached it.

Although old, its fibreglass hull green with algae and dented from various minor collisions, the boat was built for speed with a long narrow hull and high sides I couldn't see over. Hand over hand on the chrome railing, I hauled it around so the bow faced into shore. The stern was much lower, cut to accommodate the motor. There was a good foot of water sloshing about over the stained plush carpeting on the floor and swirling around the two red gas tanks. An orange anchor was lodged beside them.

I hoisted myself up over the stern and pulled on the cord to lift the motor. It was far too heavy. The keel caught the sand and the boat shuddered, the bow swinging around with the force as another whitecap rolled over, drenching me and the seats.

I looked for some kind of hydraulic mechanism to lift the prop. I glanced up at the control panel by the steering wheel. There was a bewildering display of dials, buttons, and levers — but the key was still in place in the ignition. I would have power if I could only figure out which button operated the lift. Perhaps there was a driver's manual in the dashboard.

"Megan," I shouted. "Megan."

The gulls whirled and shrieked.

I scanned the shore again for any sign of the child. I was wasting too much time. If this beach was near Hank's camp, where was his dock? From the height given by standing on one of the swivel back seats, I could see the entire length of the beach. I hoped to catch a glimpse of a small girl bent over a collection of shells or a sand castle. No one. Off to my left, though, was a cut in the sand bank that snaked back towards the woods, which seemed to pull aside for the tiniest break. A sudden wave jolted the boat and I fell into the front seat. On it, wrapped in a dingy blanket was a toy bear. Megan's bear. Hank must have her with him, and not too far away.

I jumped out of the boat and ran back through the shallows for shore. The slap of the water and the sad sight of the boat heeling over and then with an obvious effort righting itself stopped me. There was no way I was going to paddle back across the lake with Megan in the canoe. And there was no time to look for a way back through the woods. I would have to save the boat.

I stripped off jeans and underwear. I should have taken off my sweatshirt too, but the wind was brisk and I knew how cold the water was. I compromised by rolling up the sleeves and tucking its hem into my bra to try to keep it from getting soaked. I probably looked ridiculous, but there was no one to see me and I was in a hurry to get the job done.

The anchor was attached to a sturdy yellow nylon rope secured to a cleat on the stern. I pulled the bow around again and shoved the boat out of the rut its keel had dug in the sand. The waves fought to keep their prize stranded but I pushed hard and finally the boat broke free. Hoisting the anchor in one hand, I made my way to the front and grabbed the bow rope, towing the boat deeper until the water was up to my waist. I dropped the anchor. The bow swung round towards shore but the anchor held. Teeth chattering, I splashed back to the beach. I used my underwear to dry my legs, then pulled my jeans back on, stuffing the pants in a back pocket. The bottom of my sweatshirt was damp but the sun and wind together would soon dry it.

As I dressed, I headed for the break in the treeline I'd seen from the boat. It was the mouth of a creek and along its shore was a corduroy boardwalk made of short lengths of poplar nailed to longer logs to make a dry passage over the mud. The knotty branches bruised my feet. I ran as fast as I could, and as

I ran a litany repeated itself in my head: I know Hank won't hurt her, I think Hank won't hurt her, I hope Hank won't hurt her, I pray to whatever god there is that Hank is good to her.

The boardwalk became a combination bridge and dock that spanned the stream as it disappeared into the forest. I crossed over and found a well-beaten trail that led into a tunnel made by the interlocking branches of giant cedars. The ground underfoot was soft with years of fallen needles. Under the trees out of the sound of the wind, the forest was surprisingly silent. Far off, I could hear the whine of a car engine: the highway, I hoped. The land sloped steeply upwards. I ran, breath coming in great gulps, one hand pressed to the pain in my breast. I was really out of shape.

I burst through the darkness under the trees into sunlight so dazzling I was blinded. I stumbled, falling to my knees on a carpet of ferns. This was a meadow cut out of the forest, a circle of sunlight hemmed in on all sides by cedar, pine, birch, and poplar. Past the rim of grass and wildflowers that bordered the woods, the ground was littered with tiny mounds of dirt and scattered holes, a moonscape of craters whose use I couldn't fathom. Near the centre of the field was the rock cairn a settler had raised to clear the way for crops or cattle. Next to it was a tent, one of those two-person domes made of green Egyptian cotton and lightweight aluminum poles. Its door was zipped shut. Smoke from a fire pit curled up from a bed of coals. A blue enamel pot, sitting beside it on a wide, flat stone, was the focus for a cloud of insects that rose and settled with the fitful gusts of the breeze.

"Hank!" I yelled. "Megan!"

A chipmunk sprinting through the underbrush behind me paused to complain about my voice. That was the only answer to my call. Even the birds I could expect to hear were absent; silence filled the clearing, a silence centred on the tent, a silence that drew me despite myself. I didn't want to see what was in there. Stray news stories filtered through my memory, of children abducted, assaulted and murdered. To keep them at bay, I concentrated on the path, trying to step between the sharp bits of stone that littered the ground. Not just stones. I bent to examine what my big toe had nudged out of the mud: a bone, a human finger bone. Oh god. I really didn't want to look in that tent.

But I had to, of course.

"Megan?" I called again. "Are you in there, baby? It's Rosie Cairns here. I've come to take you home. Megan? Hank?"

Nothing.

I knelt at the opening. Take a deep breath, I warned myself. All I could smell was the scent of drying earth, of wood smoke and ashes, the faint tang of ooze from the marsh. I listened, but the only sounds of living creatures were my own quick breath and the buzzing of flies.

"Megan?" I whispered again. I unzipped the tent flap and peered inside.

The tent was full of a stifling blue dusky light that bathed its few contents with soft shadows. Waiting for my eyes to adjust, I felt cautiously around with one hand, still kneeling at the door, unwilling to penetrate further. An animal skin covered the floor right in front of me, its hair brittle and stiff. To one side of the door was a backpack, zipped closed but from its softness full of clothes. On the other, a cardboard box half full of cans, sealed packets of food, tin plates and cups. Three plates. Three cups. A handful of cutlery. A frying pan.

I backed out of the hut and sat up on my heels, my face turned to the sun and breeze. How good it felt. How glad I was that the tent was empty. As long as I didn't find her body, there was the chance that she was still alive. Lost and frightened, perhaps, but alive.

Assuming that Hank had taken the girl, where could they be? I climbed to the top of the rocks and surveyed the field. None of the holes looked new, the earth uniformly black and slightly steaming as the sun dried the residue of last night's storm.

"Think," I said out loud. How long had Megan been gone now? I looked up at the sun. It seemed directly overhead, a golden glaring pulse. Say it was noon — Ryan and Megan had gone down to the dock after breakfast. Megan disappeared when Ryan came up to the cottage about half an hour later. We spent another half-hour or so talking and searching for her. Say it took me an hour to reach the beach and fool with Hank's boat before finding my way here. In that two hours, would Hank have had the time to persuade Megan to come with him, bring her here, hurt (don't say kill) her, and hide her (don't say body) before taking himself off? And how would he get away?

I looked more carefully at the wall of trees. Something glinted at the far west end of the field. I shaded my eyes, squinting against the glare. It appeared to be a building of some kind.

A hard-packed trail had been swept clear of debris, skirting both fresh and dried cow patties. It led to a small corrugated iron shack at the end of a rutted lane. Its door had buckled and hung half open. I peered in. It was a storage shed, containing a hodgepodge of shovels of various sizes, an enormous pick-axe, a box of smaller trowels, several empty buckets, a stack of burlap bags, and a wheelbarrow. Looking up the lane, a track roughly hacked out of the underbrush, I recognized the glossy green of poison ivy leaves between the ruts. My bare feet were already sore and burning. This early in the season, they weren't used to hard walking without shoes. I had no idea where the lane led or how long it was before it hit either the cottage road or the highway. Looking closer, I saw something else: a set of tire tracks gouged into the soft mud as if a car had been stuck here recently and rocked free.

Just then, in one of those sudden pauses between birdsongs that shock with the depth of their silence, I heard the revving of a car engine labouring up a hill deep in the woods. Whoever had Megan was going away. Perhaps it was Hank. Or Bonnie with the police. But surely, if it was Bonnie, she would wait for me, knowing that I was coming in to the beach by water.

The quickest way back to the cottage was by boat. Hank had said so himself last night. I jumped up and ran around the field to the path that led to the beach. The waves were still rolling in, large enough now to back up the creek, flooding the boardwalk so that at times I had to feel for the logs with my toes before moving on. A heron burst out of the marsh right by my side, its huge wings pumping the air as it rose. I tripped, fell to my knees, my left hand plunging through murky swamp water deep into the muck. Leeches! I stumbled to the sand, holding my arm well away from my body until I could wash it off in clean lake water. I had scratches and insect bites galore, but nothing else.

I didn't bother taking off my jeans but plunged into the lake and waded out to the boat. I put one foot on the propeller and grabbed the motor, hoisting myself on to the transom. A wave caught the boat broadside; the sudden jerk toppled me and I fell in, swallowing lake water, coming up coughing and blue with the shocking cold. I got on board on the second try.

When I was sixteen I had spent every weekend of my holidays at Annie's family's summer cottage on Lake Huron. Her cousin Simon kept a speedboat there and we all took turns driving it while the others waterskied. That was a long time ago. And the controls on his boat had been a simple on/off switch and a gear lever.

Can't be much different than driving a car, I assured myself. I contemplated the crowded dash, then turned the key; the engine coughed, caught. I left it running in neutral and went back to haul in the anchor. By the time it was aboard and I was back in the driver's seat, the waves had pushed the boat almost into shore. I pulled the throttle full back. The motor bucked and roared; I fell backwards over the seat as the boat spun, bouncing and tipping from side to side. I scrambled back to grab the wheel and get it headed straight out into the waves. The propeller churned up a mass of sand and weeds but didn't stall the motor. I pointed the bow at the spit of land that marked the river mouth.

I angled across the waves, holding my breath every time a particularly large white cap rocked the boat, wincing every time the bow slapped into a trough. A lot of water slopped around the bottom; there should have been an automatic bilge on such a fancy boat but I didn't know how to activate it. I fought to keep the wheel steady on course. I kept the throttle at half speed, afraid to go too fast in such rough water. Still, I made it to the river mouth in minutes. Just in time, I remembered the purpose of the line of plastic buoys and made a clear course for the channel between them. Sheltered from the wind's fury by the reed beds stretching to either side, the water here was much calmer. I slowed to navigate the narrow river. Hank must have visited often to trust finding the channel in the dark. As for me, I could hardly wait to get back on firm ground and into dry clothes.

THIRTEEN

Around the next bend, the dock came into sight. Ryan was sitting there, curled in a fetal position, arms hugging his knees, head buried, his back to the cottage. He looked up at the sound of the motor, then hid his face again.

I knew at once that Megan hadn't been found. I turned the boat in towards shore and cut back the throttle. Over the sound of the idling engine, I shouted, "Is Megan back yet?"

He shook his head no.

"Your Mom? Will?"

No to both.

"Can you give me a hand? Grab the bow when I get close enough?"

He didn't move. I turned off the power and let the current carry the boat close to shore. I stretched and caught a cleat on the dock and pulled the boat in. I secured it with the bow line and got out, wincing as my bruised feet hit the boards. The current caught the stern and swung it out wide across the pool. I considered trying to tie that end to the dock as well, but shrugged. The boat wasn't going anywhere and there was no one to bump into it.

I sat down beside the boy. Here on the river in the shade of the trees, it was quite cool. I was still wet through and trembling deep inside.

"Got lonely waiting up at the house?" I asked.

He shook his head, but still wouldn't look at me.

"It's not your fault, Ryan. My cousin, Hank, came along in his boat and took her for a ride."

"She wouldn't go with him," he muttered. "She wouldn't go with a stranger."

"She's only four," I pointed out. "And she really wanted to go to the beach. If he told her he'd take her there..."

"She wouldn't," he insisted. "She's street-proofed. Just like me. She wouldn't go unless he had the secret family word."

"What's that?"

"I can't tell. It's a secret code so we know if the person really is a friend of Mom or Dad's. If they say the right words we can go with them."

"But I found her bear in the boat." I handed it to him.

Ryan grabbed the toy and hugged it close. He began to rock back and forth, back and forth. "Where is she then?"

I had to be careful. "I found my cousin's camp in the forest. His tent was empty, but they must have just left. I heard a car going up the road. They'll be here soon."

This news did little to comfort him. He rocked back and forth, clutching the bear to his chest. "She wouldn't leave T. Bear behind. She never goes anywhere without T. He used to be mine, but I gave him to her. She never, never would forget him."

There was no answer for this. I shivered. "Look at me, I'm soaked," I said, amazed myself at how chipper my voice sounded. "It's a little early to go swimming, don't you think? I fell in the lake and it was cold."

He didn't bother responding. What a fool I must sound to him, blathering on about the weather when he was so full of guilt and grief.

I sighed and stood, holding my hand out to him. "Come with me up to the cottage while I get changed, okay?"

"You can't go up there," he wailed. He looked up, his eyes wide, the pupils great dark holes. Something had scared him, and scared him badly.

"What happened?" I knelt down and took his chin in my hand so he couldn't look away. "Did someone come to the cottage when you were there by yourself?"

"No."

"Tell me."

"I can't." He shook my hand free and began that sinister rocking again.

"You'll feel better."

He didn't answer.

Frustrated and freezing, I stood again. I didn't want to leave him alone. "I have to go and get some dry things on before I catch my death of cold. You can come with me or stay here by yourself."

"Don't leave me." He began to cry, great tearing sobs.

"You have to tell me what the trouble is. I can't help you if I don't know the problem."

"I did something bad." His voice was so low that I had to lean over to hear it.

"Broke something? I'm sure it was an accident. It doesn't matter."

"Not that." He paused. "Mom told me to stay in the cottage the whole time she was gone. She made me promise."

"It's scary to be by yourself for such a long time," I assured him. "She won't be mad at you for coming down here."

"I waited and waited. Nobody came. I tried to read a book, but they're all about birds and boring stuff like that. Then I thought about the cars..." He bit his lip so hard a drop of blood welled up.

"The cars?" I prompted him.

"In the driveway. There was a car all covered up. You know what little kids are like — I thought Megan might have got inside and was hiding there. Maybe she fell asleep in the dark. She likes to find hidey holes. I thought if I found her no one would be mad at me any more."

"None of the rest of us thought of that," I congratulated him. "That was really good thinking." I remembered, though, that Will had tried the door handles through the tarp; that car had been locked tight.

He whispered, "I pulled up a corner of the blanket to look. I couldn't see in so I took it all the way off. It was real heavy. I had to climb right on the roof." He began to cry again.

"It's all right to take the tarp off. I'd have done it myself if I'd thought of it. Just because Megan wasn't inside ... "

"There was a lady."

"A lady?" I repeated. I put my arms around him. He clung to me, his face buried in my shoulder.

"I saw a fly come out of her nose." He collapsed against me in a storm of tears.

I held on to him, stroking his back, feeling the knots of bone along his spine. "There, there," I repeated over and over, as a spell against the horror. "There, there. It'll be all right."

We should never have left him alone, I said to myself. He's just a little kid. Poor guy. I held him tightly while he cried.

It must be Marilyn that he'd found. There was that blood-stain in her bed, those precious artifacts in the trunk. Whoever killed her and put her in the car must have called Hank last night, pretending to have a message for us from her so that we wouldn't go looking for her.

Ryan seemed to have settled down. I had to get him back to the cottage; I had to get changed. Surely it was time for Will to get back. I spoke softly and calmly, leaving no room for doubt in my voice.

"We're going to go back to the cottage." His body stiffened but I wouldn't release him. "We'll go in through the front. You won't see the car at all. I need you to make a fire for me while I get changed. That would be such a big help. It must be lunchtime too. Are you hungry? We can make lunch and have it ready for the others when they get back."

"What about..." he began, but I shushed him.

"Let's not talk about that right now. Your Mom will be bringing the police with her. They'll take care of everything."

"Mom will be mad at me. For looking." His voice was a little stronger now.

"No, she won't. She'll think you're a very clever boy to have the idea that Megan might be in the car in the first place. And a very, very brave boy to stay here by the dock after what you saw."

"Do you think so?" He drew back far enough from me to look me in the face. His own was bloated and red — in that he took after his mother.

"Of course. You didn't do anything wrong. You didn't run away. My goodness, what would we have done if you'd got lost too?"

I hugged him again, then stood. He stood up with me.

Hand in hand, we climbed the hill.

I winced with every step. My feet were bruised and torn from my scramble through the woods and exploration of the field. My shoulders ached from paddling. My jeans and sweatshirt clung, an unpleasant second skin through which the wind cut with a freezing blade.

Inside the cottage, I dropped Ryan's hand. He followed me into Marilyn's room and waited while I fished out dry clothes.

"You could go start the fire," I suggested.

He shook his head. "I want to stay with you."

I felt awkward about stripping down in front of the boy. Part of me told me I was being ridiculous; another part shrank from exposing myself to the child.

"All right. You can stay but you have to promise not to look. I'm a little bit shy."

"Okay," he nodded.

I hadn't brought many clothes with me for the three-day weekend. The pink shirt and jeans I had on yesterday were still damp from last night's trip to the cars. I had shorts and another short-sleeved blouse. I wished I had brought more warm clothes. Bonnie might have something. I went into the bunk bedroom, Ryan still at my heels. Bonnie's big white sweater hung off the end of the bed. I put it on.

"That's Mom's sweater." Ryan said.

"She won't mind. Let's get that fire going."

I huddled as close to the flames as I dared. It was long past noon. Will should be here any moment. I glanced at Ryan. His head was nodding, eyes closed.

"Let's sit on the sofa," I suggested.

Still clutching the bear under his arm, he joined me there. He wasn't far from sleep, exhausted by the stress of his vigil on the dock. He stretched out, his head pillowed on my lap, face turned to the fire. In minutes, he was breathing deeply and evenly, fast asleep.

I edged out from under his head, placing a cushion there. He muttered and rolled over, but didn't wake. I waited a few minutes to make sure, then stoked up the fire. I needed a drink. There wasn't much left in Bonnie's scotch bottle, but I poured one hefty belt and downed it. It burned my throat, but finally stilled the trembling that had shaken me since I found the toy bear in Hank's boat.

One of the kitchen cupboards held an assortment of household medications: bandaids, mercurochrome, aspirin, even a bottle of pink cough syrup. The sink counter was not too high. By balancing on one foot and leaning most of my weight on that hip, I could lift the other into the sink and rinse it off under the cold running water. My soles were such a mess of blood and dirt that I could barely look at them. The mercurochrome stung. I fit bandaids over the worst cuts and lined the insides of my socks with tissues. I was afraid that shoes would pinch my feet too much; in fact, the rubber soles cushioned them enough to make walking possible, if still a bit painful.

I would have to go and look at what was in that car. I didn't exactly doubt Ryan: his fright was too deep-seated not to have been triggered by something truly horrible. But he was only a child; perhaps he'd misinterpreted what he'd seen. Perhaps Marilyn was preparing some kind of exhibit that required a mannequin. That would make sense of the contents of the trunk under the bed as well: she'd need them to complete the display.

I limped down the trail. A blue jay flitted across the clearing in a flash of colour, squawking all the way. Two crows quarrelled from tree top to tree top, their harsh caws grating on my ear. I could hear, too, the faint buzz of a car coming along the lane, fading as it dipped between hills but definitely coming closer. Will was returning at last. At least I hoped it would be him.

He had been right about Marilyn having a sports car. It was an MG, hunter green with a hard top and North Carolina plates. The consulting business must pay well.

I leaned heavily on the roof. Ryan must have had quite a struggle pulling the tarp off; in fact it still covered the tiny trunk. I squinted against the glare of sun on glass, took a deep breath, and peered in.

Eyes met mine, eyes wide open, all whites, the pupils rolled back into the lolling head. Her long hair lay bunched against the pane, matted with something the flies had found and clearly loved. She'd been stuffed in quite roughly; her sweater had pulled up under her armpits, and her long pants were shoved up to bare her shins. Her knees had been bent so that one bare foot was pressed against the windshield while the other was lodged under the dash.

She was clearly beyond help. I backed away and sat on the hood of the Ford. My legs wouldn't support me any longer.

Poor Ryan. Poor little boy. Poor me.

I put my head between my knees, breathing deeply. I was sure it must be Marilyn in the car. Who else could it be? I had found my cousin at last, too late. If only time could be set backwards to last night when Will and I had been down here together. If only I'd sent Bonnie and the kids home in the rain instead of letting them in. If only my aunt hadn't decided to heal the family wounds. If only ... if only ... if only ...

FOURTEEN

A car pulled up beside the Ford. Doors slammed.

"What's wrong, Rosie? Are you all right?" Will called at the same time as Bonnie shouted,

"Where's Ryan? What have you done with Ryan?"

I pulled myself to my feet, my back to the MG and its terrible occupant. "Ryan's up at the house. Did you find Megan? Where's the police?"

"They're not coming," Bonnie said. She raked her hand through her hair, pulling it back from her scalp so sharply that she winced. "I've got to see Ryan. I'll tell you everything in a minute."

She ran up the hill to the house.

I looked at Will. "What's going on? Why aren't the police on the way? How come Bonnie's with you?"

"I met her on the road just this side of the highway. She was trying to run, but could barely keep on her feet. I couldn't get a word out of her the whole way in, other than that Megan was missing and she'd gone to telephone at the store. That's all she'd say."

"We've got to get the police," I said.

"What's happened?" Will caught me as I started to sink to the ground again.

"Look in there." I gestured at my cousin's car.

Will's sharp intake of breath told me he'd seen the body.

"Who is it? Marilyn?"

"I guess so. She doesn't seem real to me. What I mean is that we never actually met and now we never will." I laughed unsteadily.

Will tried the door handles. "Locked."

"Just as well. Ryan found her first. At least he just caught a glimpse of her. If he'd opened the door and she'd fallen out on him..." I shivered. "As it is, the poor kid's in terrible shape. He was hysterical when I got back. He seems better now. He fell asleep and I came down to look."

"Got back from where? Where did you go? I thought Bonnie's car had run out of gas."

"It has. I took the canoe to the beach. I thought maybe the current might have carried Megan down river, if she'd fallen in."

"You haven't been in a canoe in ages."

I rubbed my sorest shoulder. "Tell me about it. I had to, though, there wasn't any choice. I found Hank's boat stranded on the beach with Megan's teddy bear in it."

"And Megan?"

"Not there or at his camp in the woods. He must have taken her, though Ryan swears she wouldn't go with a stranger."

"It couldn't have been Hank," Will objected.

"What do you mean? It had to be his boat and his tent. Remember he said he was camping out close by? Who else could it have been?"

"It might have been his camp, but he wasn't there," Will insisted. "I saw him when I left. There was a commotion going on at the store, so I stopped to see what was the matter. The old man had a heart attack and they were taking him to hospital by ambulance. I saw Hank get in with the stretcher."

"Then who took Megan?"

Will couldn't answer. After a moment, he bent to tug at the tarp. "Let's cover this up again," he suggested. "It seems indecent to leave her exposed like this." He heaved it over the little car's roof.

"You don't think the same person ..." I couldn't finish.

"Let's go talk to Bonnie." Will pulled me to my feet and put his arm around my shoulders. "She'd better have a good reason for not calling the cops. We're in way over our heads here."

He pulled me away towards the path to the back door.

I stopped suddenly. "I bet it's Roger Markham."

"Markham? Why would he take her?"

"Gianelli said they were looking for him as well as for Marilyn. And Mr. Ross implied that he had suspicions about that survey and Marilyn wanting power-of-attorney. Bonnie told me that Markham spends a lot of money. What if he assumed Marilyn was going to inherit the property and made some kind of deal with her? Maybe then she decided to back out. She's an archaeologist, right? Maybe she found the relics and said the land couldn't be developed until the site was properly excavated and he got mad and killed her and..."

"Slow down, Rosie. You're getting carried away."

"But it makes sense. Megan would go with him; he's her uncle."

"But why would he take Megan in the first place? And how would he know where to find Hank's boat?"

I scuffed at a stone in the path with the toe of one shoe.

"Besides," Will went on, "the property belongs to you. Even if Marilyn had found those relics and was going to turn the site over to the authorities, it's you Markham would have to negotiate with, not her."

"But with her out of the way ..." I paused and began more slowly, picking through the plot. "He could have killed her by accident. He came by boat, but was going to take her away in the car. Only he heard us coming down the road and had to take off. He could have known about Hank's boat because Marilyn took him to see the site in it. And he could have taken Megan to blackmail me into giving up the land."

Will shook his head. "That's a lot of could haves and maybes."

"Have you got a better explanation?"

"No."

"Well, then?"

We went back up to the cottage. Ryan was awake, crying in his mother's arms, but softly now, not with those wild hiccuping sobs that had come with his first telling of the story.

Bonnie stared at us over the top of his head. Her eyes were nearly invisible between red swollen lids, face a clown's mask of blotchy circles and pallid skin, hair pasted to cheeks and neck with tears and sweat. She must have tripped on the road in her hurry: the knees of her pink sweat suit were stained with grass and mud.

"Ryan's told you?" Will asked.

Bonnie nodded. "I should have taken him with me." She nuzzled him with her chin.

"Why didn't you call the police?" I demanded. "Aren't you worried about Megan?"

"Megan's all right," Bonnie said.

"All right?" The three of us spoke together, Ryan raising his head to look at his mother. Will continued, "How do you know?"

"I spoke to her. On the phone." She caressed her son's hair, gently wiping the tears from his cheek with her palm. She spoke directly to him. "She's fine, really. She'll be back here this afternoon. In just a little while."

"But how..." I started.

"The cops ..." Will interjected.

Bonnie held up her hand. "We can't call the cops. He said if there was any sign of police, he wouldn't bring her back."

"Who said?" I asked. "Was it Roger Markham?"

"Why would Uncle Roger take Megan away?" Ryan asked. "He doesn't even like her."

"That's not nice," Bonnie reproved him. "What am I saying?" She rubbed her eyes. "No, I don't think it was Roger. Though he has a car phone and I could hear traffic in the background."

"What does he want?" Will asked.

"I talked to Megan first. She sounded fine, only worried that she's lost T. Bear." Bonnie tried a little laugh. It didn't sound amused.

"I've got him," Ryan displayed the toy proudly. "Rosie brought him home."

Bonnie looked at me.

"It was in Hank's boat. I found his camp too, but it's empty." I limped over to one of the easy chairs and sank into it.

"What's wrong with your feet?" Will asked, following me. He sat down on the wide arm.

"A long story," I shrugged. "Come on, Bonnie, get on with it. And what do you mean you talked to her on the phone?"

"Just that. There was a message for me at the store to call a number if I wanted to speak to Megan, so I called and I did. She's fine, really."

"Who gave you the message?" Will asked. "I saw Mr. Cook being taken away in an ambulance and Hank was with him."

"It was some woman. Smith I think she said her name was. Meryl Smith." She tossed her head. "What difference does it make?"

"What was she doing there?" I asked.

"What is this, an interrogation?"

"We just want to know what happened," I snapped. "I've been worried sick about Megan."

"Okay, okay." Bonnie sighed dramatically. "The pay phone was out of order. I went inside to ask if I could use their private phone. Some woman was there, tending the store. She said the old man was sick and she was filling in, as a favour, until Hank got back. Anyway, she had a note for me."

"Who from?" I blurted, just as Will asked, "How did she know the note was for you?"

"She asked me right away if I was Bonnie Hazlitt. I guess they don't get too many strangers coming into the store at this time of year. When I said I was, she gave me a note and told me I could use the phone in the kitchen."

"Where's the note?" Will stretched out his hand. "Let's see it."

"I don't have it."

"What?"

"I shredded it, okay? I was so upset, I didn't know what I was doing. I just wanted to get back here in time."

"In time for what?" It was my turn to question her.

"Before he arrived."

"Who?" I practically screamed.

"The man who's got Megan. And no, I don't know who it is."

"Calm down, both of you," Will said. "What did this Meryl Smith woman say about the person who left the note?"

"I didn't think to ask her."

"You didn't think?" I demanded.

"I was upset, okay? I wasn't thinking straight at all." She glanced down at Ryan. He wasn't paying any attention to her, but was busy fooling with the bear, tying the red ribbon around its neck into a series of elaborate knots.

Will sighed. "I guess you don't remember the phone number? There'll be no way for the police to trace the caller?"

"We're not involving the police," Bonnie snapped.

"When we have Megan back," I soothed. "Then they can look for him."

"You know I can't have the police around." Bonnie hugged Ryan.

"I want to go home," he said. "Really home. I don't like any of this."

"Don't I have enough to deal with, without getting into this again?" Bonnie whined. "Everything I do is for you, you know that."

Ryan turned his head away without answering.

"Let's get back to Megan," I suggested. "This woman gives you a message with a phone number for you to call..."

"And when the phone is answered, it's Megan," Bonnie continued. "She didn't say very much, other than wanting her bear. And wanting to go home," she rolled her eyes. "Then this guy takes the phone away from her and tells me that if I call the police, I'll never see her again. That he's watching and will know if any strange cars come down to the lake."

We all looked towards the windows. I wished there were curtains, blinds, anything to cover up those blank, transparent squares.

Bonnie fished a tatty kleenex from inside the sleeve of her shirt and blew her nose. "I'm not about to take chances with my daughter's life."

"Who is he? What does he want?" Will repeated. I squeezed his hand. After a moment, he squeezed back.

"Relics," Bonnie stated flatly.

"The artifacts we found?" My voice squeaked. "But how does he know about them?"

"I don't know. But that's what he wants. He says if you'll give them to him, he'll give back Megan."

"What about his voice?" I pushed her. "Did you recognize it? Was he young? Old?"

She shrugged. "I couldn't tell. The line was terrible, all static and fuzz. Mrs. Smith did tell me something interesting, though."

"I thought you said you didn't talk to her?"

"Not about the note. I didn't want to tell her anything about that, I was afraid she might go to the police. But she saw I was upset when I was leaving. She wanted to give me a cup of tea." Bonnie giggled wildly.

"What did you say to her? How did you explain what was going on?"

"I told her that I was running away from my husband, that he beat me up..."

"That's not true," Ryan shouted. "Dad never hit anybody."

"I had to say something," Bonnie soothed. "It was the only thing I could think of. I told her the phone number was my lawyer's. She was very understanding. She said Hank had run away from his folks too, before he came to live with his grandfather. But that's not all. When I said that I'd met Hank down here at the cottage, she told me he was real close to Dr. Finch. That he'd worked for her last fall on a dig down south." She leaned back against the cushions, then winced and tugged at the back pocket of her sweatpants. "She gave me this."

"What is it?" I reached for the tattered paperback.

"It's a guide for students helping out on an archaeological site."

I thumbed through the pamphlet. There were pictures of tools like the ones I'd seen in the shed in the woods, and diagrams of excavation pits. "I wonder if this comes from the site she's accused of looting?"

"Maybe Hank stole stuff from there too, and Marilyn was taking the blame for him. They're cousins, after all, and she probably has more chance of defending herself than he would," Will suggested.

I held up a smudged photograph of a field pockmarked with craters. "The clearing where I found Hank's tent looks just like this."

"That trunk of relics you found must have come from there." Bonnie's voice rose with excitement. "The survey must have identified that field as an archaeological site. Hank dug up the relics and was storing them here until he found a buyer. He had a key, remember? You came before he could fetch them. He must have figured taking Megan was a sure way to get you to give them up."

"You think it's Hank who has her?" Will asked.

"Of course. He would be desperate to get the artifacts. They're worth a lot of money for a kid like him if you know the right people to sell them to. That's why he was nosing around the museum, looking for leads. What did you find exactly? Pipes? Jewellery?"

"Both of those," I nodded. "And a bag full of bones."

Bonnie whistled. "That's what he wants then. I know," she jumped up. Ryan sank back down against the arm of the couch. "Your cousin found the relics dug up and brought them here. Hank came after, they argued and he killed her."

"Don't, Mom," Ryan pleaded. "Don't talk about her." His lips trembled.

Bonnie put her arm around him. "Okay, Champ." She looked at us, but nodded. "That's what must have happened," she whispered.

I shook my head. "Couldn't be. Hank was at the store when we stopped there, so he couldn't have been here then. And if he killed her, you'd think he'd show some sign of that. He's too young to hide his emotions that well and to pretend that she's still going to turn up. Remember: he told us about the phone call from her friend, that she was going to be late arriving."

"A lie to keep you from getting suspicious," Bonnie suggested.

"Besides," Will added. "He couldn't have Megan. I saw him get into the ambulance with his grandfather about the time you say she disappeared."

Bonnie sighed. "Well, whoever it is, he wants those relics."

"Are you sure you didn't recognize his voice?" I asked.

"He hung up as soon as he said what he wanted." Bonnie took the bear from her son and unwound the ribbon, smoothing it out between her fingers. "What difference does it make, anyway?" She looked up, suddenly frightened. "You wouldn't keep those things hidden, would you? You will help me get Megan back?" Her voice trembled.

"Of course we will," I said. "It's not right to sell them, but as long as Megan is in danger, I don't see what choice we have."

"Unless we can figure out who's got her and come up with a plan," Will pointed out.

We sat in silence for a few minutes. Bonnie kept glancing at her watch and then back to the door.

Will finally spoke again. "Maybe Rosie's right about Roger Markham. Maybe Marilyn wanted to report the site to the authorities once she realized what was there. Roger was afraid of wasting time and losing out on his deal; he'd be happy to bulldoze all that history into the ground. Then again, she knows what the artifacts are worth; maybe she thought she could exchange them for what she'd sold down south, or use them to pay for her legal costs. If she did that, she wouldn't have to sell the land. They had an argument and he killed her."

"That makes more sense," I agreed. "Except that I'm the one who owns the land, so I would have to make decisions about the site. Killing her wouldn't get him any closer to getting legal access to the deed. And why would he take Megan?"

Before anyone could answer this question, Ryan jumped up.

"Listen," he said. "I hear a car."

Will strode to the back door. "Someone's coming," he said.

"Megan!" Ryan ran to the back door.

"Come back here," Bonnie shouted.

He stopped and turned around.

She lowered her voice, "I don't want you to get into any trouble."

"What do you mean?" The boy reluctantly returned to his seat. Bonnie grabbed his hand and squeezed. "He might have a gun."

"We should do something," I insisted. "Not just wait here like sitting ducks for whoever-it-is to tell us what to do."

"I'll see if I can find a knife." Will rummaged through the kitchen drawers.

I picked up the poker and went to stand on one side of the hall entrance, hidden from the view of anyone coming in the back door.

"Don't," Bonnie pleaded. "If you try to stop him, he won't tell us where Megan is. I won't get her back."

Will slammed the drawer shut. "We'll make him tell us." He ran his finger along the blade of a fish gutting knife. "This is plenty sharp."

Bonnie's voice rose, "Don't be crazy, Will. Hank or Roger

or whoever will be desperate. He's got nothing to lose after kidnapping my baby. Someone will get hurt and I'm afraid it will be her."

I lowered the poker. "She's right, Will. We'd better just give him the trunk and be done with it. Once we've got Megan, we can contact the police. Once they know who, and what, to look for, he won't get far."

"Thank you, Rosie," Bonnie said. She brushed away tears.

"He's coming," Ryan whispered. He sank down, peering over the back of the sofa at the back door.

I reluctantly returned to my chair by the fire. It needed stoking. I was crouched in front of it when the back door crashed open.

"Hello," Hank carolled. "Everybody home?"

FIFTEEN

He didn't look very frightening. His eyes were red and his hair had come loose from its elastic binding and hung in long black greasy strings on either side of his face. His denim jacket was unbuttoned; he wore the same sweatshirt and jeans he'd had on the day before. Over one shoulder dangled an empty canvas backpack.

The gun in his hand, though, meant business. He waved it at Will. "Go and sit with your wife," he ordered. "I want you all where I can see you."

Will grimaced, but did as he was told.

"And you can put that poker on the floor and just scoot it my way," Hank continued. "Best to keep temptation out of reach."

"Where's Megan?" Bonnie hissed. "What have you done with her?"

"She's all right," Hank grinned.

"You've got her?" I burst out. "Why?"

He spoke to Bonnie. "You told them what I want?"

She nodded. "Rosie said you can have them."

"Good."

"What I can't figure out," Will interjected, "is how you managed to be in two places at once: with your grandfather in the ambulance and abducting that little child at the same time."

Hank smirked. "I have friends, you know." He stepped

further into the room and caught sight of the booklet lying on the coffeetable. His brow furrowed.

"Where did that come from?" he demanded. "How did you get hold of it?"

"Mrs. Smith gave it to me," Bonnie said. She was leaning towards Hank, her eyes wide, staring.

"Mrs. Smith?" He was clearly puzzled.

"The woman tending the store for your grandfather." Bonnie enunciated every syllable, her tone flat. I looked at her curiously. She was trying to convey a message to someone, but I couldn't decide whether it was to us or to Hank.

"You're lying. You were snooping around in my house."

"I was not."

"You had to. To find this."

"Why would I lie to you?"

"Stop it, Mom," Ryan cried. "Stop fighting. You're always fighting."

"Keep out of this, Ryan," Bonnie ordered. She tried to shove him down on the seat, but he wriggled away and stood at the end of the sofa, arms crossed, staring at her.

She softened her tone. "I'm upset, honey. I'm worried about Megan."

"If you hadn't brought us here, none of this would have happened," he accused her.

She looked stricken. I crept over to put my hand on her shoulder, to comfort her. She shook it off.

"Don't say that, Ryan," she pleaded. "I feel so bad about all this. Don't make it worse."

"Megan and I didn't want to come with you. We like our house. We like living with Daddy and Lynne. We said so, but you wouldn't listen. You never listen."

He ran across the room. Hank caught him and held him at arm's length so the boy's whirling fists wouldn't touch him.

"Let go of me, Hank," Ryan yelled.

"Let him go." Bonnie screamed.

Hank did.

"I hate you," Ryan said. "I hate all of you." He ran into the bedroom and slammed the door behind him.

Bonnie put her face in her hands and began to rock as I'd seen Ryan rocking on the dock hours ago. "I can't stand any more," she cried. "I just can't stand any more."

"Should I go to Ryan?" I wondered aloud.

"Only place you're going," Hank said, "is to get me my trunk. Where is it?"

I gestured to the other door. "In Marilyn's room. Under the bed."

He giggled. "You've got to be joking. She had the stuff under the bed all along?"

"Didn't you know it was there?" Will asked. "Aren't you the one who put it there in the first place?"

Hank ignored him. He pointed the gun at me. "Go and get it. And don't try any funny stuff or you'll never see Megan again."

"All right, all right." I edged around him and went into the bedroom. He backed down the hall, so that he could keep an eye on Bonnie and Will in the living room while, at the same time, he could check on me. From the bunk bedroom came the sound of sobbing. Everyone ignored it.

I knelt down and felt under the bed. We hadn't pushed the trunk in very far; I caught the handle right away. I leaned back and pulled. It scraped along the floor.

"I can't pick it up," I told Hank. "It's too heavy."

"Drag it out here, then."

I did as he said, crawling backwards on my hands and knees and pulling it along behind me. The metal bands on its corners carved furrows in the soft wood floor.

"Where's the key?" Hank asked. He was practically dancing with excitement.

Will took it from the bowl on the mantel where he'd put it for safekeeping earlier.

"You go get it," Hank ordered me.

When Will handed me the key, our hands touched. He held my fingers for a second and smiled. I tried to smile back.

"Open it, open it," Hank gestured with the gun. "I haven't got all day."

Even Bonnie was curious about the trunk's contents. She knelt on the couch, her hands clasped together, leaning forward to see what had endangered her daughter. All that could be seen was the quilt.

"We'd better take that too," Hank said. He let his pack slide to the ground and nudged it towards me with his foot. "Put everything in here. And be careful."

The quilt provided a cushion on the bottom of the canvas bag for the other objects. One by one, I brought them out and packed them in: the newspaper-wrapped pieces of pottery, the shoeboxes of arrowheads and pipes, and the two store gift boxes, one rattling slightly as the corn kernels shifted in the pot, and the other full of beads, rings, and the shell necklace.

"I don't think there's room for this," I said to Hank, pointing to the blanket-wrapped parcel of bones.

"What is it? The skeleton? Leave it."

"That would be worth something," Bonnie piped up. "To a collector, I mean. If the whole skeleton is there, that is."

"I don't care," Hank said. "I'm not going anywhere with a bunch of bones on my back. It's not respectful."

"Respectful!" Bonnie hooted. "Aren't you the one to talk."

"Be quiet," he ordered her. To me, he added, "Leave those bones on the bed. After we've had time to get away, you can call the police. They'll get them back to the people they belong to."

"What people?" Bonnie demanded. "Those bones are ages old."

"More reason to take care of them," Hank retorted. "Besides, I'm not touching them. No way."

"That's the lot, then." I folded the ends of the quilt over the treasure and pulled the drawstring tight. "It's wrong to do this, Hank. These things belong in a museum, or with whatever tribe lived here once."

"They're all gone, dead, departed. This stuff is no good to anyone but me. I need the money. Now that Grandad's gone, I'm getting out of here. I'm not wasting my life in a two-bit store in the middle of nowhere."

"He died?" I burst out. "Your grandfather died?"

"Yeah." Hank tossed his head. "Doesn't matter."

"I'm sorry," I said. "What happened?"

"Heart attack. That smart-aleck lawyer came around looking for Marilyn and got him all riled up about the survey."

"Roger Markham is up here?" Bonnie asked. She nodded at Will and me. Markham's presence at the lake confirmed our theory that he had killed Marilyn.

"Yeah. Said he was looking for Marilyn, started ribbing the old man. Said she," and he pointed at me again, "would sell the land to her cousin, no problem, and then they'd be able to go ahead with development. You should of heard Henry curse; that old man had a tongue on him." Hank allowed a little smile, then sobered. "I got him to the hospital too late."

"I am sorry," I repeated.

"None of your business. You should have kept away altogether. All you've done is cause trouble."

"It's not my fault," I said, standing. "Beatrice Baker contacted me. I didn't go looking for her."

"We're wasting time," Bonnie broke in. "I want Megan back. Why don't you just take those things, all of them, and give her to me."

"No way," he shook his head. "Not the bones. I'll leave them for her," he pointed to me. "She owns the land now, until Marilyn gets her to sell. Where is Marilyn anyway? She should be here by now."

"Don't you know?" Will asked.

"Know what?"

"Give me Megan," Bonnie interrupted. "You've got what you want. Now you have to keep your side of the bargain."

"All right," he ordered. "This is what we'll do. You three will sit here for two hours. Then Megan will come back."

"How?" I asked. "Who'll bring her?"

"That's my business," he said. "You just sit."

"Let me come with you," Bonnie pleaded. "Don't make me wait any longer. I can't bear it."

Hank put his head on one side, considering. He was grinning again, in control and revelling in the power. "Okay. And you better bring the boy too."

Bonnie jumped up. "Oh, thank you." She turned to us. "You'll do as he says, won't you? You'll wait here for a couple of hours?"

"Sure, Bonnie," I hugged her. "You go and get Megan."

"Ryan," Bonnie carolled. "We're going to find Megan. Come on, honey."

The door opened. Ryan stood there, the bear still under his arm. "Are we going to go home then? To Ottawa?"

Bonnie ruffled his hair. "Let's worry about that later. Don't you want to see your sister?"

"Yeah." He pointed at Hank. "Do we have to go with him?"

Bonnie glanced back and forth between the two. "Just till we're with Megan."

"I don't like him," Ryan stated. "He's mean."

Hank grinned.

Bonnie sighed. "It's not a matter of liking. Now, help me with our stuff. You take the sleeping bags and I'll take the packs."

"Why don't you leave all that here and come and get it later?" I suggested.

Bonnie hesitated. "We might go straight on," she said. "Once Megan's safe." She shivered. "I don't think I can stand to spend one more minute in this place. I'm sorry, Rosie."

"You can't just leave me in suspense like this," I protested. "I have to know that Megan's safe."

"I'll leave a message on your machine, okay? You can phone home for it in a couple of hours."

"Promise?" I pleaded.

"Sure. Don't worry. Everything will be fine now."

Before I could add anything else, she darted into the bedroom and came back out with her arms full of sleeping bags and packs.

"Come on, Ryan," she pushed him towards the back door.

He refused to move. "I won't go out there. Not by that car."

"It's all right," Will quickly assured him. "It's covered up. You won't see anything."

"What's to see?" Hank asked. "A couple of old cars."

"Come on," Bonnie said. "Megan's waiting." She hustled the boy out the door.

Hank waved his gun at us one more time. "You listen to Bonnie," he said. "You wait right here. Two hours."

Then he followed them out the door, banging the screen behind him.

"Well," said Will.

"Yes. Well." I crossed the room. He stood and we hugged. I could hear his heart beat, sure and steady.

We heard two car engines start up, one right after the other.

"Did you give Bonnie the keys to our car?" I asked Will.

He patted his pocket, shook his head no.

"That's funny," I said. "She couldn't get her car started earlier."

"Hank must have had a jug of gas in his car or truck. He helps run a service station, remember."

"How would he know to bring it?"

"Could be just standard out here in the country to carry an extra five gallons of gas. That would be enough to get her to the highway and the station."

"Or maybe Mrs. Smith told him Bonnie'd had to walk to the store."

"You know what was funny? Hank didn't seem to recognize that name when Bonnie mentioned it."

"I noticed that too."

We listened to the diminishing whine of car engines.

"Where do you think Megan is?" I continued. "Do you think he left her alone all this time or with that friend he says did the kidnapping? I can't figure out why she'd go with a stranger. She's so shy; she must be frightened half to death."

"He could have tranquillized her."

I shivered. "Poor little kid. I don't think he hurt her, though, do you?"

"He wouldn't dare take Bonnie with him, if he had."

"How long do we have to wait?"

"They've just left."

"I wish we knew for sure that Megan was all right. I think it's really selfish for Bonnie not to bring her back here."

"Bonnie's pretty upset." Will tapped his watch face. "Stopped again. I'm going to have to get a new battery."

"Not as upset as I'd be, though, if it was my little girl gone missing."

"What would you have done? If you called the police, you might never see her again. Besides which, Bonnie isn't exactly free of kidnapping charges herself."

"She said she'd think about taking them home."

"Yeah, well... You say she's always complaining about money. How in the world does she think she's going to support those kids on the run?"

I flopped down on the sofa. "I don't know. She said she had

some money coming in. She's been doing a lot of contract work lately, word processing and stuff like that at home."

"Wouldn't think there'd be enough money from that."

"You'd be surprised." I sighed. "To change the subject, what are we going to do about Marilyn?"

"Not much we can do for a while. She'll keep."

"How can you be so flippant?"

He smiled at me. "How can you not be? This whole day has been beyond bizarre. What time is it? Only four o'clock? It ought to be midnight."

"Do you know what I just realized? I'm hungry. I can't believe it. You'd think food would be the last thing on my mind."

"Want some chili?"

We both burst out laughing. Once I started, I couldn't seem to stop. I could feel tears seeping from my eyes. Will hugged me again as the crying began.

"It's all over now, Rosie," he murmured. "Bonnie will be with Megan soon and then she'll work out with the kids what to do. Hank's gone. The police are looking for Markham and once we tell them about Marilyn, they'll lock him up for good."

I took a deep breath, and let it out slowly. "I wish Bonnie had left Ryan with us and brought Megan back here. He didn't want to go with Hank. I could see how reluctant he was, couldn't you?"

"Almost as if he knew him."

We were both silent, thinking. Will went into the kitchen. He opened the fridge and began to hand out cheese, butter, and a round of paté.

"Should we go after them now?"

Will shook his head. "We said we'd wait. If they're still at the store and they see us, it could mean trouble for Megan."

"I'm not very good at waiting," I complained. "I keep thinking about that poor little kid..."

"I think we should wait at least one hour, if not the two." He put the food on the table. "Why don't you slice up that loaf?"

I got the bread and went to work on it. Will popped open two cans of beer and handed me one.

"Okay, let's go through the whole thing," he said. He began to number points on his fingers. "First, Markham and Marilyn

assumed she would inherit the property and made plans to sub-
divide it for cottages. Then, they found the grave site."

"You're assuming it was Marilyn and not Hank who found
it?"

"For the moment. Marilyn knew what the artifacts were
worth, and she knew who to sell them to. They plunder the
field as soon as the frost is out of the ground."

"I can't imagine Roger Markham with dirt on his hands."

"Let's say they made a deal with Hank. He obviously wants
to get away from here. Maybe they said they'd split the profit
from the sale with him. Or that he could have the artifacts and
they'd get the land."

"Okay. Then what?"

"Beatrice dies and they find out that you inherit the land,
not Marilyn. Markham tries to buy it from you, in her name,
but you won't sell until we've had a chance to come up here."

"And when we decide to come right away, they have to hide
the artifacts instead of selling them."

"Right. Marilyn arranges to meet you here, and gets rid of
me by saying that she wants to get to know you. Markham
would turn up 'by chance.' Between the two of them, they figure they can persuade you to sell them the land. Then they'd
be home free."

"So why did Markham kill Marilyn? Without her, he has no
claim on the land at all. I might sell the land to my cousin, but
I'd have no reason to share the profits from development with
him."

"That's true." He scratched his beard.

"I wish you wouldn't do that," I said. "It really bugs me."

"What?" He pulled his hand away.

"You always scratch your beard when you're thinking. It
sounds like sandpaper on plywood."

"Sorry. I'll try not to do it any more."

"Sure. Until the next time." I grinned at him.

"You have your little annoying habits too," he countered.

"Like what?"

"Twirling a lock of hair until it's wound tight, then letting it
spring open. Over and over and over."

"I do not." I dropped a strand of hair that my fingers somehow had got tangled in.

It was Will's turn to grin. "Maybe we're going at this from the wrong angle," he suggested. "Maybe it wasn't Markham who killed Marilyn. What if Marilyn didn't know about the site until she found the relics already dug up? What if she took them from the shed and hid them here? The looter came after her and killed her."

"Hank? From the way he was talking, he doesn't know she's dead."

"Who else knows the value of native artifacts? Who else needs money?" Will paused. "Did you notice that Bonnie kept trying to change the subject every time we got close to telling Hank about finding Marilyn's body?"

"That was because she didn't want to remind Ryan of what he'd seen."

"Maybe."

I buttered a slice of bread. "We're supposing two crimes here," I said. "That Hank or a friend of his took Megan to force us to give him the artifacts; and that Markham killed Marilyn in a fight over the land."

"Right." Will began to put a sandwich together.

"We take as given that Hank doesn't know Marilyn's dead?"

His mouth full, Will nodded.

"And he himself couldn't have taken Megan because you saw him up at the store on his way to the hospital. So she went with a stranger?"

"Mm-hmm."

I drank some beer. "Bonnie knew what the artifacts were worth."

"Bonnie?" Will repeated. He put down his sandwich.

"It makes sense. A sick sense, but this whole thing is sick. Look at it this way: we both got the impression that Ryan knew Hank. What if Hank was one of Robin's street kids? Maybe the one Harold objected to being there at the house when Megan and Ryan came for Thanksgiving last year? What if Hank told Bonnie and Robin about the site? She knew about this place because she'd been here with her brother-in-law years ago, so she knew that Mrs. Baker was old and unlikely to come north before summer. There'd be time to dig and get away before anyone came. She knew what the relics were worth and she probably could find out who was buying. She had those magazine articles I told you about, remember?"

"And she needs money to start a new life..."

"Exactly. Bonnie persuaded Robin to help Hank loot the site. She probably told him that they'd use the money to start a new life together. I know they've been fighting a lot lately, because he's been working so hard. Some of that time, he must have been up here, digging. Then Aunt Beatrice died and it looked like Marilyn was going to sell the land. Only it's my land. And we were coming to see it."

"Robin comes up to get the loot from the camp and finds it missing. He comes around to the cottage and finds Marilyn... "

"Who's innocent of the looting, but wants the relics to sell to help pay for her legal fees. She won't tell him where they're hidden; they have a fight; he kills her; panics when he hears our car coming; and hides her body in her car under the tarp."

Will carried on the story. "He takes the boat back to the camp and calls Bonnie from the store."

I interrupted. "She would just have heard from Harold about his marriage and his offer to her to take the kids for the long weekend."

"Right. She grabs the kids, and comes here to see if she can find the treasure before we do. It's a real bonus for her that you're neighbours and so she has an excuse to visit. And when she realizes we've found the relics, she comes up with another plan."

"Bonnie wouldn't kidnap her own daughter, would she?" I realized what a stupid thing I'd just said. She'd done that all right. Twice.

"Megan would go with Robin without any trouble," Will was still working it out. "And Robin could have been waiting with her in the car the whole time Hank was in here with us."

"How could she know that Megan would be alone at the dock? She couldn't count on Ryan coming up to the cottage."

"That's when things started to go really wrong. It was bad enough that Marilyn had been killed..."

"I'm sure that was an accident. Robin's a very gentle person."

"They must have argued," Will agreed. "And he's a big man. He could have knocked her over and her head hit one of those bedpost knobs. That would account for the blood on the mattress."

"They would have been in the room to get the trunk ... "

"Or he might have cornered her in there. If they knew where the trunk was to begin with, they wouldn't have had to go through the whole rigmarole of the kidnapping."

"True. But that still doesn't explain why he didn't take both kids."

"He was probably supposed to take both. I'd gone and wasn't expected back for a few hours. Bonnie would send you out in the canoe or off in the woods to look for the kids while she looked for the trunk. Once she had it, she'd be off in her car to meet with Robin and the kids at the store."

"But then Ryan got left behind and she'd run out of gas."

"It would have looked pretty strange if she'd insisted on taking the boy with her on the long hike up to the highway. He would have slowed her down."

"So the phone call was a fake." I shook my head. "And Mrs. Smith is a fiction. I mean, there are no neighbours out there on the highway. She must have made it all up. She must have searched the house to find that book of Hank's. He was right about that. She missed her calling. She should have been an actress."

"She had the sleeping bags all rolled and their bags packed. She wasted no time getting out of the cottage with Ryan as soon as Hank had the relics. She must have told Hank to bring the gas for her."

"And once they were gone, we would have been left trying to explain how Marilyn's body got in her car."

"We've been set up."

"Come on." I put my sandwich down. "They haven't had much of a head start."

"And if we catch up with them?"

"We stay with them until we get a chance to call the police. Maybe if Bonnie sees us and realizes we know the truth, she'll give herself up."

"Hank has a gun," Will reminded me.

I was already out the door. "He won't use it," I shouted back. And added, under my breath, "I hope."

SIXTEEN

The cow gate had been left wide open. As Will slowed to pass through, I unbuckled my seat belt ready to get out to close it.

"Don't bother," he said.

"But the cows?"

"What harm can they do? They can't open doors."

He gunned through and down the drive through the tunnel of trees. The lane was in deep shadow. I blinked when we came out to the river clearing.

Will jammed on the brakes.

I braced my hands against the dash, rocking in my seat with the sudden stop. "What the hell?"

"Look."

The bridge was a scene of confusion. On the far side a white sedan was stuck in the mud, its engine roaring as its driver attempted to rock it free. Behind it was an Ontario Provincial Police cruiser. On this side, two vehicles were stopped nose to tail: Bonnie's Ford in front and a blue pick-up truck behind. They were both empty.

A small crowd stood in the centre of the bridge. When Will turned off the motor, we could hear Bonnie cajoling and threatening as her hands flew about to illustrate the explanations and persuasions that Joe Gianelli, facing her, clearly wasn't buying.

"What's he doing here?" I said.

"Who is he?"

"Detective Gianelli from Toronto. That must be Wilson in the car." A uniformed OPP constable was also on the bridge, listening to the conversation, her hat tucked under her arm. Every few minutes, she brushed at the flies that swarmed around the bright yellow crown of her hair.

Ryan was standing beside his mother, the ubiquitous teddy bear under his arm. Behind them were Hank and Robin, the latter carrying Megan who seemed to be asleep.

"We were right," I said. "It was Robin who took Megan."

"A set up," Will growled. "Bonnie has a lot of explaining to do. And some apologies as well."

The car was unmarked, but had an offical look. It gave a great roar and lurched backwards out of the rut, almost colliding with the cruiser behind. The constable ran back to move her car. Gianelli turned away also as the others prepared to return to their cars. When she saw us, Bonnie faltered, then shepherded her children towards their vehicle. "Hurry up," I heard her say. "Get a move on."

"Wait a minute," Will roared. He was out and running down the lane, slipping on the mud and keeping his balance by luck. "Don't let them get away."

I was right behind him. "Megan's all right, isn't she?" I demanded. "She's been all right all along. There never was a kidnapping."

"Don't say anything, Rosie," Bonnie pleaded. "Trust me, okay?"

"Trust you!" I stopped, astonished. "I've trusted you long enough."

"What's going on here?" Gianelli asked. "What are you talking about? Who's been kidnapped?"

Wilson got out of his car. His hand rested on the pommel of the gun he wore at his belt. The constable also turned.

"This is ridiculous," Bonnie snapped. She turned to Gianelli. "We're in a hurry, I told you. We want to get home before dark."

"I want to get down," a small voice piped up. "Put me down."

Robin lowered Megan. She ran to Ryan and tugged at the bear.

"Gimme," she ordered. "Mine."

"You left him behind. Finders keepers," Ryan said.

She stomped her foot. "Gimme," she wailed, her voice rising. "Mine, mine, mine."

"Give her the toy, Ryan," his mother ordered. Her voice was weary.

Ryan glared at her, but handed over the bear. Megan clutched it to her breast and stuck her tongue out at her brother.

"Did you see what she did?" he demanded. "Tell her to stop, Mom."

"Give us a break, Ryan. Megan's only a little kid."

Ryan kicked a stone into the water. "You always let her have her own way," he whined. "It's not fair."

"Nothing's fair," Bonnie snapped.

"Maybe the kids should wait in the car," Will said. His voice was grim.

"Get in the car, Ryan, Megan," Bonnie ordered.

"I don't want to," Ryan pouted.

Bonnie's voice rose. "You get in the car when I tell you to."

Tears slipped down his cheeks. "You're mean. I hate you."

She raised her arm. "You do as I say or I'll give you something to cry about."

"Bonnie, what are you doing?" I shouted at her.

She looked at her raised fist and then at her son. Her face crumpled. She lowered her hand. "Just do it, okay?" she said to the boy. "Just this once, will you do as I ask. Please?"

"Come on, Megan. We know when we're not wanted." He took his sister's hand and dragged her to the Ford. She stumbled along behind him, clutching the bear. We were all silent until the car door slammed.

"I'm sorry, Rosie, Will," Robin said. "It wasn't supposed to turn out like this."

"Shut up," Bonnie spat. "If you'd done your part properly, none of this would have happened."

"What's going on?" Gianelli repeated. He slapped at his neck. "God, the bugs are bad up here."

"It's spring," the constable said. "What do you expect?" She looked the lot of us over, her eyes narrowing. "I'm Constable Lisa Lachance, OPP. I was showing these fellows the way to the

Baker place. City types like them, sure to get lost on these back roads and cause us even more trouble, having to find 'em."

"He's got a gun," I said, pointing to Hank.

"A gun?" Both officers reached for their weapons, Lachance's hand to her belt, Gianelli's disappearing inside his jacket.

"I do not," Hank said. His face was white. "It's not real. It's plastic."

"It looked real," I objected.

"Where is it? Hand it over." Lachance circled the group, edging closer to the boy.

"It's in the truck, on the seat. You'll see it's a toy."

Lachance leaned in the truck window and brought out the weapon. I flinched.

"He's right." She tossed it in the air and caught it in one hand. "It's a good replica. Perhaps you could explain what you're doing with it?"

Before he could answer, Wilson joined the group. He held his hand out to Will and introduced himself. "We're here to talk to Dr. Marilyn Finch."

"You're a little late," I said. "She's dead."

"No!" Hank shook his head violently. "She went back home. He told me." He jerked his thumb at Robin.

"Look," Bonnie interrupted, her voice barely under control. "Will you just let us go? I want to get the kids home to the city. To a bath and a decent night's sleep."

I ignored her. "I'm sorry about Marilyn, Hank."

"You're lying," Hank said. "She can't be dead."

"Who's dead?" Gianelli said. "One of you at a time." He pointed to me. "It's your cousin we're looking for. You say she's been killed?"

I nodded. "Her body's in her car, back up at the cottage. But I think she was killed in her bedroom. There's blood all over the sheets."

"You killed her," Hank turned on Robin. "You bastard." He flung himself on the other man, knocking him to the ground.

Wilson and Lachance jumped in. They separated the two men, Wilson twisting Hank's arm cruelly up behind his back. The boy hung from his grasp, sobbing, blood pouring from the nose that Robin had smacked hard. Robin got to his feet slowly, dusting off his trousers. He shook off the constable's helping hand. Gianelli quietly moved up beside him, not touching him yet, but close enough to put a hand on him if necessary.

"It was all her idea." Hank mumbled through his tears. He pointed with his chin at Bonnie.

"Liar," she hissed. "I don't want to listen to any of this nonsense. Come on, Robin. We're leaving."

"Marilyn's the only one who's ever been decent to me," Hank continued. "She gave me a job, she gave me books to read. Mr. Elgin, pal to the lost boys," he jeered. "All you cared about was her," he pointed to Bonnie. "You'd do anything she told you to."

"You shouldn't say anything more till you get a lawyer," Robin advised. "You don't want to get yourself into more trouble. You know what will happen to a boy like you in prison?"

Hank began to weep. "I thought you were my friend," he cried.

"Oh, God," Bonnie said in disgust.

"Bonnie," Robin warned.

She shrugged. "What's the use? It's all going to come out. You might as well confess and get it over with. And let the kids and me go." She stared hard at Robin.

"Me, confess?" He turned away from her.

She put her hand on his arm and leaned close to him. "You know my brother-in-law's a lawyer," she said. "He'll help you get out of this. For my sake."

"Roger Markham?" I almost laughed. "He's on Harold's side. Why would he help the two of you?"

"Because Harold would rather sell his soul than see the mother of his children in jail," Bonnie said. "Besides, it's all Robin's doing. Not mine."

Robin just looked at her.

Will shook his head. "I don't believe this," he said. "What would Robin know about Indian artifacts? He's a social worker. You're the one who works at the museum."

"Besides, Roger Markham isn't going to be much help to anyone, least of all himself," Gianelli added. "He's under arrest, charged with embezzlement. His uncle turned him in. Seems things weren't quite right with the Baker papers, among others. That's why I was so interested in meeting him at the house the day Mrs. Baker died. Mr. Markham has been a matter of some interest to me for a long while."

"He was here this morning," I said, remembering Hank's story of the argument that had precipitated Henry McDonnel's fatal heart attack.

"He was arrested in Barrie just before noon, apparently heading for the city and then the border," Gianelli said. "I came up with Pete here to have a talk with Dr. Finch. He has some questions to ask her about her aunt's death and I want to know what hand she had in the paper work that Markham was arranging. They were close, those two, practically brother and sister, according to his wife."

"Ellen would say anything that leaves her out of it," Bonnie said. "Especially if she thinks Roger is in serious trouble. I bet he had contracts signed with some developer who thought he already owned the land."

Gianelli nodded. "You're right about that part of it. That's why he was helping Dr. Finch try to force Mrs. Baker into giving her complete control of the property through power-of-attorney —they could have sold the land right away. But then the old lady died..."

"Was it an accident?"

"No," he grinned at Wilson, then quickly covered up his triumph with a frown. "My hunch proved right. She was pushed. One or both of our suspects visited her recently; their fingerprints are on the stair railings and on her desk. I figure they got into an argument when they were going through the Cook papers she had stored in a room at the top of those stairs. She was probably going on and on about making things up with you. Could have been manslaughter," he shrugged. "They'll probably argue that, anyway. Doesn't matter. We've got two cases solved here in one go. It's good for the books, eh Pete?"

"Poor Aunt Beatrice," I said.

"He must have been furious when she fell," Wilson put in. "If they'd been able to sell the land before she died, it wouldn't matter what her will said."

"So they planned to get me alone up here and force me to sell the land to them," I shivered. "I don't like to think how they were going to do that."

"That's when Marilyn found the relics," Will said. "When

she came up here to set the scene for you."

"And Markham came after her," Gianelli summed up.

"But he didn't kill her," Will continued. "Rosie and I have been talking this over. We think we know who did that."

"Of course Roger did it," Bonnie snapped. "She was trying to hold out on him, on account of the relics."

"It was you all along," I accused her. "That's why you were so anxious to come up here. You had this planned: bringing the children here and taking the artifacts. It's how you were going to finance a new life with them. You and Robin and Hank were after the relics; Marilyn just wanted the land. What happened? Did she find the trunk and hide it here? And then one of you — Robin, I bet, he's been out of town a lot this week — got into a fight with her about it? And killed her?"

"It was an accident," Robin cried. He held his hands out to Gianelli in appeal. "I didn't mean to hurt her."

"Don't say anything," Bonnie ordered.

Robin opened his mouth, then closed it.

"You had an argument? You acted in self defence?" Wilson goaded him.

He muttered, "I tried to reason with her. I told her why we needed the money, so we could take the children and start a new life together. It's all for the children. Her children."

"You bastard," Hank strained towards the other man. "I loved Marilyn. You knew that. I was going to give her my share, for her law suit. She needs the money now that she can't sell the land."

"Why didn't you call the police?" Lachance interrupted, trying to defuse the boy's anger and to encourage Robin to continue his story. "If it was an accident..."

"I was going to, but Bonnie wouldn't let me. She said you wouldn't believe it was an accident and that we'd get into trouble over the relics. Especially the bones. I was going to move the car later, but I didn't get the chance."

"What bones?" Gianelli demanded.

I wasn't about to get sidetracked.

"You set up the kidnapping of Megan after I told you we'd found the relics," I accused Bonnie. "That's why you were out so early — meeting with Robin. How could you put me through that? I was frantic for Megan. And what about Ryan?

He was terrified for his sister and sick with guilt. And horror, too. What kind of mother are you?"

Bonnie looked up then. I recoiled from her glare.

"What do you know about motherhood?" she snarled. "You're so full of advice, know-it-all. I'm sick of you. All of you." She turned her back on us.

Hank chose that moment to make his getaway. He kicked Wilson hard in the groin. Wilson screamed, folding into himself, falling. Hank whirled and shoved Lachance hard. Her arms flailed as she fought for balance, her feet slipping on the wet boards. Hank didn't pause; he elbowed Bonnie viciously as he charged past her. I saw her clutch one breast and grimace with pain.

And then he was off, racing up the road towards the cottage.

"Stop," Gianelli yelled. "I'll have to shoot." He unbuckled his holster and pulled the gun half-way out.

"Don't," I said, reaching for his arm.

Hank hesitated as he reached our car. He turned around, his right hand slipping inside his jacket as if he was reaching for something.

"Watch out," Bonnie screamed. "He's got the real gun in his belt."

All of us, except Gianelli, ducked. Noise erupted: the shot roared louder than seemed possible, loud enough to drown the sudden eruption as birds rose in panic from the bushes along the river; loud enough to drown Hank's cry and my own scream; loud enough to leave in its wake a silence that drummed on the ears, holding us all in the pause between heartbeats, before our breaths came back, and then the tears.

Lachance limped up the road towards the body that lay sprawled in the muddy tracks. Gianelli leaned over the bridge rail and vomited into the water. He wiped his mouth, and looked over at us. Bonnie was on her knees beside her car, whispering to the children who could not be seen. Robin had fallen to his knees and was weeping into his palms. Will and I held on to each other, neither of us able to speak.

"I didn't mean..." Gianelli began. "He shouldn't have run."

"S'okay, Joe," Wilson put his hand on his partner's arm. "You didn't have any choice. Give me the gun, eh?"

Gianelli dropped it. It hit the wooden planks with a clang, spun around and stopped, the barrel pointing at Bonnie. I suppressed a giggle; it was too much like a mad game of "spin the bottle," the prize here a final cold kiss.

Lachance straightened up and came slowly back towards us. She didn't look at Gianelli. "I'll have to call it in," she said.

"He's dead?" I whispered.

She nodded, biting her lip. "Anyone know his next of kin?"

"I guess that's me." I began to tremble. First Aunt Beatrice, then Uncle Henry; Marilyn's corpse in the car; Hank in the dirt: all the Cooks and Bakers were gone, leaving only me who never had belonged as the last of them.

"What about his weapon?" Gianelli asked.

"There wasn't one," the constable answered.

"But you all saw him reaching for something," Gianelli protested.

I turned on Bonnie, but she was faster. "You've done it now," she accused him. "Shot him right in front of my kids. I hope you're satisfied. I hope now you'll let us go."

"It was you," I began, but Gianelli didn't wait to hear what I had to say.

"I thought he had a gun," he repeated, his voice dull. "I saw him reaching..."

"That's enough," Wilson interrupted. "Let's leave it for the SIU. That's the Special Investigations Unit," he added softly, to us. "They'll have to take a look at this."

"Shit," Gianelli groaned. "I think I'll go sit down, if you don't mind." He shrugged off Wilson's hand and trudged over to his car. He sat in the passenger seat, feet outside on the ground, head in his hands.

"It's all your fault," I said to Bonnie. "You're not going to be able to twist your way out of this one. Hank was just a kid, he didn't do anything wrong but panic and run."

"I thought he had a gun," Bonnie retorted. "He showed me one earlier when we came out to the cars. That toy was for Ryan."

"Stop lying," I said. "We know the truth. Robin's admitted that he's the one who killed her."

"Give me a break, Rosie," Bonnie answered. "It's so obvious why Hank ran. He knew he wasn't going to get away with it.

Robin was just trying to cover for him, that nonsense about an accident." She pulled on the car door but it didn't budge.

I imagined the two children inside, crouched on the floor, still so terrified they would not let even their mother in.

"Ryan? Megan? Open the door for Mommy." She rattled it angrily, then hit the car roof with the flat of her palm. She turned back to Wilson. "When can we go?"

"Not just yet," Wilson said. "You're going to have to make a statement about what went on here. This kidnapping that Mrs. Cairns referred to. And Dr. Finch."

"What's to say?" Bonnie's sigh was nearly a shriek.

"Your friend here," Wilson nodded at Robin, "has just confessed to murder. As well as the kidnapping: two kidnappings, am I right? Does their father know where the kids are?"

Bonnie didn't answer that last question. "I'm not responsible for what *he* does," she spat, pointing with her thumb at the man who, still on his knees, was rocking back and forth, hugging himself.

"Bonnie," Robin looked up. He'd taken his glasses off to wipe his face with his sleeve. Unframed, his eyes were red-rimmed and vulnerable. "It's gone too far."

"Shut up," she hissed. "Think of the kids."

"You're not doing a very good job of that," I said. "Look what you've dragged them into."

"You keep out of this. Interfering bitch." She shoved me aside and stalked over to Robin, standing over him, hands on hips. "Come on, Robin. Tell them you were lying to protect that little creep. They'll let us go."

He shook his head. "It's too late. That boy is dead and it's our fault."

"Your fault, you mean." She turned away from him. "I knew I should have come up here and taken care of it all myself. I knew I shouldn't trust you to get things right."

"How can you say that?" Robin lurched to his feet. "I've done everything for you. I even killed for you." His voice broke.

"That's enough." Wilson said. "You're both under arrest, for kidnapping and murder."

Lachance rejoined us on the bridge. "Help's on the way," she reported. "I asked them to send a social worker too. For the kids."

"What do you mean, for the kids?" Bonnie snapped. "They stay with me."

Lachance shook her head. "No, ma'am, not until we get this all sorted out. The kids need someone who can help them deal with trauma. It's not an easy thing, seeing someone killed."

Bonnie glared at Wilson.

"He had to," the detective defended his partner. "He warned him, you all heard that. You all saw that kid reaching for something. How was he to know that he didn't have a weapon?"

Lachance ignored him. "We'll be calling their father. I assume you can give us his number so he can come get them?"

"Can't they at least drive back to the city with me?" Bonnie cried. "Can't I have that much more time with them?"

The two cops shook their heads. "Sorry."

Bonnie started to cry. "I only did it for them. To be with them."

"Great job you did too," I snapped.

She glared at me.

Lachance gestured at the car. "You can talk to them until the social worker gets here. You've got some explaining to do to them."

"You mean I'm actually allowed to speak to my own children?"

"If they want to listen to you."

Bonnie tossed her head. "Of course they will." She strode back to her car and banged on the glass. For a moment, nothing happened, then Ryan peeked up over the edge of the dash. "Come on," Bonnie said. "It's all right. You can come out now."

After a long moment, the door opened. Ryan stepped out, clinging to the handle, his eyes darting from Robin to the two policemen, to Will and me. He avoided looking up the road. I couldn't blame him. Megan followed, the baby blanket tucked around her like a shawl, T. Bear clutched under her arm.

When they reached their mother, she hugged them fiercely. "I'm sorry. I only wanted us to be together."

"Are we in trouble? Are we going to be arrested?" Ryan asked.

"No, no," Bonnie said. She stroked her daughter's hair

away from her eyes.

The little girl hung back. "Are we going home?"

"Sure you are," Lachance said. "Your Daddy's going to come and get you soon."

"You mean really, really home?" she asked again.

"Really," she smiled at the little girl.

"Is Mom coming with us?" Ryan asked.

There was an awkward silence punctuated by Bonnie's sniffs as she tried to hold back her tears.

Wilson's voice was gruff. "You can sit together in the cruiser until it's time to leave."

"Is that a good idea?" Lachance objected. "It's against regulations."

Wilson shrugged. "So where's she going to go? We'll need a tow truck to clear the way out of here."

Bonnie took the two children by the hand and led them across the bridge. She looked back at me once before ducking into the back seat. I looked away.

"Come on," Wilson said to Robin. "You can wait in our car. Just leave Joe alone, though, okay? He won't want to be talking to you." He grabbed Robin roughly by the elbow and steered him over to the sedan. Gianelli didn't even look up as the car rocked with Robin's entrance. The back door slammed and Wilson returned to stand beside us on the bridge.

Constable Lachance showed me the gray blanket she had tucked under one arm. "I'm going to cover him," she said, pointing up the trail. "Do you want see him? Before the others get here?"

I looked at the still form lying in the trail, arms and legs splayed wide as if grasping the earth, ready to push himself up and away. The birds had begun singing again and the flies had returned to cloud about our heads. The image of Marilyn's face came back to me, the flesh squashed against the glass, the flies, as Ryan had told it, crawling from her nose.

"I can't," I said. "I'm sorry."

She nodded. "That's okay. I'll just be a minute."

We watched her. She stood silently beside Hank's body as if she might be praying before shaking the blanket out of its folds. It settled gently over him. She bent to tuck one corner over one outflung hand.

Wilson blew his breath out in a long sigh. "It's going to be tough on old Joe," he said. "He's never fired his gun before. Not that I know of. Not at someone. It's hard to believe he actually hit him."

"Bad luck then," Will said.

"Yeah." Wilson scuffed his shoe. "Bad luck all round."

"About Marilyn ... " Will began.

"Let's save it for the OPP," Wilson said. He straightened up. "What are these artifacts you've been talking about, anyway?"

"Indian relics," I said. "They must be in the truck."

"More likely Bonnie's car," Will put in. "After all this, I doubt she'd let them out of her hands."

He was right. The canvas backpack was in the Ford's trunk.

Two cruisers squealed to a stop behind the other one. Four cops tumbled out, all men, all but one in uniform. Lachance made her report. While one constable paused to talk to Gianelli, the others followed her up the road.

Wilson came back to join us. "It's going to take awhile before we can leave: the OPP will have to go through the car and the cottage collecting evidence before they move the bodies. And the SIU is on its way: you'll have to make a statement about Joe."

"Things got out of hand," Will said. "He couldn't help it."

"A shame, though," Wilson shook his head. "It's not good for his record."

What about Hank? I wanted to say, but I held my tongue. What was the point in adding more recriminations to what Gianelli was obviously feeling. It was too late to help Hank now anyway.

A station wagon joined the line of cars in the driveway. The woman who got out was short and plump, her hair a halo of gray curls. She wore a hand knit sweater over slacks and carried two toy teddy bears. The OPP constable pointed to the cruiser. The door opened and Bonnie got out, her arms tight around each child. She spoke to the woman quietly, then knelt to kiss her children. They let the social worker take them back to the wagon. There was a few minutes of confusion while the constable helped direct the car to turn around in the limited space of the lane.

Bonnie stood watching until it disappeared up the road. The constable touched her arm and pointed to one of the newly arrived cruisers. She walked stiffly to it, ignoring Robin who tapped frantically on the window as she passed Gianelli's car. The constable unlocked the back door. I thought for a moment she would resist getting into the cage, but she didn't. Now that Ryan and Megan were gone for good, she had nothing left to fight for.

"What about us?" I asked. "Are we free to go?"

"Well, sure," Wilson said. "After all, you're innocent, right? Mere bystanders."

Much, much later, peace returned to the marshes. The birds had come in to nest as usual, disregarding the commotion as police milled around the driveway, the bridge and the cottage. Bird song and chatter nearly drowned the revving of car engines as trucks appeared to tow the Ford and pick-up away from the bridge. We talked to a series of officers, uniformed and plainclothes. They were all very polite, very formal.

I walked beside Hank's body when they carried him up the hill to the hearse. At least, I comforted myself, he would be with the only two people whom he had loved, his grandfather and our cousin. The three would lie in the local hospital and then I would arrange for them to be buried together.

Finally, they all left — the police, the morgue attendants, even the local reporters who'd heard the news and came rushing, looking to scoop the big city papers. Will persuaded the cops to send them away. I stood in the screened porch, listening as the last car's noise faded in the distance and staring over the marsh at the pattern of moonlight on water. The loon cried out.

Will put his arms around me and I leaned back into his embrace.

"It's beautiful here, isn't it?" I said. "In spite of everything. I can understand why Aunt Beatrice didn't want to let it go."

"What are you going to do with it?"

"I don't know just yet. I'll look into turning it over to the province. It's what my grandfather wanted all along."

"It would be a shame to see it ruined by development," Will agreed.

"And I can't bear to profit from all these deaths," I said. "I never expected to gain from going to see Aunt Beatrice. I only wanted to find my family."

"The Cooks, the Bakers, the McDonnels," Will murmured into my hair.

"The line stops here," I tried to joke. It wasn't very funny.

We listened to the lap of little waves against the dock down below and the whisper of the ceaseless breeze through the reeds.

"Those poor kids," I sighed. "Ryan and Megan. Caught between their father and mother, both of them using the kids to hurt the other."

"They'll survive."

"You think so?"

"In one way or another. We all grow up."

"I wish there was something I could do for them."

"They have what's-her-name, Lynne. The new wife. Megan said she made her father laugh. She might be just what that family needs to hold it together."

"I still can't get over Bonnie. My friend."

"She only wanted to do what she thought was best for the kids."

"Best for herself, you mean. She wanted everything: Robin, the kids, money... You heard her, she was lying right up to the end, she even tried to use Hank's death to get away. She must have thought the rest of us were pretty stupid. I was stupid enough in the first place, listening to her, letting her in. I wonder how many of those stories she told about her marriage were true."

"It's impossible to figure out relationships from the outside, what really goes on inside families." Will hugged me a little tighter.

"I have no family any more. For real, this time. I'm the only one left."

"You've got me," Will said.

I turned into his embrace and we kissed.

"We'd better go," he said at last. "It's a long drive."

"Not to the city," I said. "I want to go home with you. To sleep in our own bed. In our own house."

Even when our car crested the last rise before turning towards the highway, even when Will stopped the car to point out the lake shimmering below in the moonlight, I never looked back.

Printed in the USA
CPSIA information can be obtained
at www.ICGtesting.com
JSHW082208140824
68134JS00014B/501

9 780889 242579